Enemy Betrothed

The Billionaires' Club Series: Book 3

AE Moran

The Invisible Publishing Company

The Billionaires' Club Series

Contents

Chapter 1: Melody

I step onto the balcony overlooking the lavish mansion ballroom. I stop at the gilded banister railing and look down at countless people socializing, dancing, and enjoying the refreshments at the formal gala.

All the women wear expensive evening gowns, but only a few wear gowns as magnificent as mine.

Diamonds and precious gems stud my embroidered bodice and tight corset. This dress would look like it came from the seventeenth century, but it's been tailored in a modern style to give it a slender profile. The tailoring only makes it look even more magnificent.

I love standing here listening to the surge of voices, the tingle of glasses and cutlery, and the music drifting up from the ballroom floor down there.

I could stand here and watch all night, but I have to go down there and meet everyone.

My brother Asher stops at my side and holds out his arm. "May I escort my lady to the ball?"

I laugh at him and wind up blushing. "If you insist, gallant prince."

"I'm not your prince. I'm your brother, but you might get lucky and meet your prince tonight." He turns to look out at the guests as we glide down the sweeping staircase to the ballroom floor. "There are some pretty rich guys here."

"There are some pretty rich guys here and they all have dates," I correct. "Anyway, I'm not looking for anyone."

"Maybe you should be. You aren't getting any younger, you know."

I make a face at him. "I'm only twenty-five."

"That's a ripe marriageable age. You would be considered an old maid in any other time in history."

"I'm not in any other time in history. Anyway, I'm already engaged. No one here is rich enough to draw me away from the man I love."

"You're so picky. No one is good enough for the precious princess."

"No one but my fiancé, you mean."

We have to cut off our conversation when we get to the ballroom floor. People surround us to greet us, shake our hands, and tell us what a fabulous party my father is throwing for everyone.

I see a bunch of guys from The Billionaires' Club here. Some of them come toward me smiling. They try to talk to me, but I brush them off when I see them hitting on me.

A few of the duller ones even try to talk to me about my father's business—like I care enough to get involved in all of that.

All that billionaire stuff is so boring. It's just a big playground sandbox all the little boys play in. What girl in her right mind would want to get mixed up in that?

Asher tries to step in and answer their questions on my behalf. He downs several glasses of champagne before the evening gets started.

I hear him talking way too loudly. He's oblivious when the other billionaires' expressions go cold. They listen to him talk, but anyone can see them closing up to him.

He's technically a member of The Billionaires' Club, too, but only because he's my father's son.

Asher helps my father in his business—or he's supposed to help my father in his business. I don't keep track of it well enough to know what either of them does.

I've overheard the servants talking when they don't know I'm listening. They all think Asher is a joke. They think he's obnoxious and spoiled—and I can't argue with that.

My father loves Asher too much and gives him everything he wants. My father only involves Asher in the business because Asher wants to be involved in the business.

For all know, my father gave Asher the money so he would qualify as a member of The Billionaires' Club. It wouldn't surprise me. My father has given Asher more than that and lived to regret it.

I'm just looking around for my father so I can make a tactful escape when Giovanni Nowaczyk glides over to me smiling like the cat that ate the canary.

Giovanni's reputation with the ladies is unmatched. He might as well walk around wearing a neon sign that says, *Chick Magnet.*

Women flock to him because of his money. He takes advantage of them and discards them just as fast.

I see Giovanni coming a mile away. That gleam in his eye tells me exactly what's going to happen next.

He eases up to me standing way too close. If Asher was any kind of brother worth the name, he would step in and push Giovanni away from me.

Asher doesn't notice. He's already starting on his sixth glass of champagne and talking to Rory Kahn about some deal Asher claims he's about to cut.

Rory stands in front of him listening with a totally blank expression on his face. Asher doesn't even notice that Rory isn't responding to anything Asher says.

"So what is a knockout like you doing in a dive like this?" Giovanni murmurs in my face.

"I'm waiting for my fiancé to show up, so you can take a step back and mind your manners, Giovanni. No one is interested."

"Oh, plenty of people are interested. Plenty of engaged and even married people are interested. You don't have to stop living your life just because you're engaged or even married." His eyes dip to my cleavage and his eyebrows jump. "You look stunning. Where has Saul been hiding you all these years?"

"Far away from you, I'm sure, and all the other scumbags like you."

"Scumbag!" Giovanni bursts out laughing. "I'm flattered, Melody! I didn't know you cared!"

Fortunately for my sanity, my fiancé Taylor Erwin shows up right then. He comes up behind me and slips his arm behind my back.

I gasp when I realize who it is. I want to exclaim in relief that he's finally here, but he doesn't look at me. He levels Giovanni with a knowing glare.

Taylor isn't a member of The Billionaires' Club, but he knows Giovanni's reputation as well as anyone. Taylor would have to be dead not to. Everyone knows about Giovanni.

Taylor's eyes say it all. "Am I interrupting anything?" he asks. He already knows he is.

"Giovanni was just leaving," I reply.

Giovanni grins up at Taylor. "You have a very beautiful fiancé, Erwin."

"I know I do," Taylor mutters in a voice of pure ice. "Don't let me catch you stepping out of line around here."

"I would never step out of line with a lady who was spoken for." Giovanni looks back and forth between us grinning like anything. "You two have a lovely evening. It was delightful to meet you again, Melody." Giovanni nods to Taylor, says, "Erwin," and walks off into the crowd.

I wait a respectable amount of time before I turn to Taylor. My hand flies to my forehead. "Oh, thank God, you're here!"

He frowns at me. "Did he do anything to you? He better not have. He thinks his money can get him anything he wants. I bet it won't get him out of jail."

"He just wouldn't shut up and leave me alone even after I told him to. He's such a player!"

"Forget about him." He pulls me into a quick hug and keeps one arm around my shoulders to turn me away. "Come on. Let's go find your father."

We head off through the crowd. I don't see or hear anyone around me. I don't want to be here all of a sudden.

It will always be like this. I can't even show my face in public without guys trying to hit on me.

They all want to get into my father's pocket. Every eligible bachelor in New York wants to land Saul Gottlieb's daughter.

They think hooking up with me will give them instant access to my father's giant import/export empire.

Some of the guys from The Billionaires' Club are the worst. Very few of them are as bad as Giovanni and some are really nice.

Then there are the one or two bad apples who think that we're somehow made for each other because they're in the club and my father is in the club.

The announcement of my engagement to Taylor didn't help anything. If anything, it made these hounds even more rabidly horny to break me and Taylor up.

I breathe a sigh of relief when I see my father in the crowd. He's talking to Dante Helme, an older, grey-haired member of the club.

Dante is nothing like my aging, shrunken, wrinkled father even though they aren't that far apart in the same age.

Dante obviously works out—a lot. He takes outstanding care of himself and it shows. He looks like he just stepped off the cover of GQ.

He wears his grey hair combed back and gelled into a sporty backward swoop. His white beard and mustache come to a point under his chin. Any woman would melt for him. His age only makes him more attractive.

He's always been impossibly sweet to me. He never steps out of line even once. I won't have to worry about anything if I go over there while he's talking to my father.

Taylor leads me over there, shakes hands with both of them, and both my father and Dante hug me and kiss me on the cheek.

"You look smashing, Melody," Dante tells me. "Did you design that dress yourself?"

I blush at him. "Stop trying to flatter me. I couldn't design a dress like this."

"I've never seen anything like it. It's so fresh and unusual. It looks incredible on you."

I blush again and look away. My father changes the subject. "Did you talk to your people about the warehouse situation?"

They launch into a discussion about some business deal they're doing. I barely listen to the details.

I get distracted by one of the waiters going past with a tray of champagne glasses. Taylor notices. "Do you want something to drink?" he asks.

"That would be great."

He kisses me on the forehead and disappears into the crowd. He leaves me there with my father and Dante.

"We still need to meet with both our legal teams to iron out the details," Dante is saying. "Nothing happens until we do that."

"Of course," my father agrees. "We're just talking here."

"Oh, look," Dante exclaims. "Niko Holloway is here."

My father's expression darkens. "What is he doing here?" he snarls.

"Don't be like that," Dante counters. "I want you to talk to him."

Dante raises his arm to wave at someone. I turn around to see who it is.

I've heard of Niko Holloway, but I don't know him. He's one of the youngest members of The Billionaires' Club. He might even be the youngest.

This is the first time I've seen him in the flesh. He's five-foot-ten and built like a ton of bricks. Short, curly brown hair tops his head and he narrows his flinty brown eyes to survey they room.

His presence instantly changes the atmosphere in the ballroom. I don't know why, but he sends a charge of electricity shooting through the air.

My father lunges for Dante and pulls his arm down. "Don't call him over here!" my father hisses. "He shouldn't even be here!"

"Why?" Dante asks. "He's one of the biggest players in the club. Anyone would be lucky to work with him."

"He screwed me over on a business deal in the past and stole a whole bunch of money from me," my father husks. "I didn't even invite him to this party. I don't know why he's even here. Stay here. I'll call security to throw him out. Then we can go on with our discussion."

Now it's Dante's turn to hold my father back. "Stop right there, Saul. I don't know what your history with Niko is, but you better get over it real quick. You can't throw him out. He's a member of the club in good standing. You humiliating him in public would be disastrous for you. It wouldn't affect him, but no one in the club would do business with you again—and that includes me."

My father freezes and his eyes go wide staring up at Dante. "What did you just say?!"

"I said I won't do business with you if you don't treat Niko with the respect he deserves. He's here because I invited him."

"*You* invited him?!" My father's voice starts to rise. "He's a snake! He doesn't belong under my roof!"

Dante clamps his hand on my father's arm in a death grip. "I invited him here to include him on this deal. Niko runs the biggest trucking network in the country. We would be stupid not to include him. You either do business with him or I'm out. Those are my terms. Take them or leave them. You deal with both of us or neither of us."

He says it with such finality that I see my father shaking. He wilts in front of Dante and my father's hands fall away from Dante's arms.

Dante pulls free, but he doesn't stop glaring at my father. Dante sure knows how to drive the nail into the coffin.

He finally pries his hands off my father's arms, turns around, and waves across the ballroom. I can't look as I feel Niko's presence approaching from the other side of the room.

He leaves a wake of commotion in his path as people hustle to get out of his way. His reputation precedes him.

He's a shark. He might be the biggest, deadliest shark in The Billionaires' Club. The press says Niko has never failed in any business venture he has ever pursued. He knows how to pick them, and when he does, he goes for the jugular.

I've never heard of him screwing anyone over before. I definitely didn't know he screwed over my father.

I don't pay enough attention to my father's dealings to keep track of that anyway. If Niko crossed my father, my father never told me about it—not that he tells me about his dealings anyway.

Niko stops next to me. His presence radiates a kind of predatory power at me—except that he doesn't even see me. He locks his gaze only on Dante.

I've never encountered anyone like Niko before. Just having him standing next to me burns me with unbelievable ferocity.

He vibrates with unknown possibilities—like he might explode any second now—and yet he stays perfectly calm no matter what.

He and Dante shake hands. "How you doing, man?" Niko asks in a hushed undertone.

"Thank you for coming." Dante waves at my father. "You and Saul Gottlieb know each other, don't you?"

Niko narrows his eyes again when he turns to stare at my father. "Yeah," Niko murmurs. "We know each other."

My father glares straight back at him, but my father doesn't make the same impression. My father trembles before Niko.

I might be the only person standing here who recognizes those trembles as the result of rage, but it only makes him look like he's shaking in his shoes in front of Niko.

Dante changes his tone to a harsh snap. "We're going to do this deal and make a ton of money. I expect you two to bury the hatchet and make it work so we can all ride off to the bank with our profits. Is that clear? I don't want to hear any drama from either of you. Whatever happened in the past is gonna stay there. I expect both of you to behave as perfect professionals."

"You won't have any problem with me, man," Niko murmurs, but he never takes his eyes off my father. "If anything goes wrong in this deal, it won't come from me."

"What is that supposed to mean?!" my father snaps. "Are you accusing me of something?"

Niko shrugs. "You said it, not me."

"That's enough!" Dante interrupts. "Let that be the last time I hear any remarks like that from either of you. This deal doesn't go through without all three of us. If you piss me off, I'm out. Do you got that?"

Niko finally tears his eyes away from my father. I can't even tell what Niko is looking at. He doesn't seem to be looking at Dante anymore, either.

"Don't worry, man," Niko murmurs in the same deadly undertone. "Nothing will go wrong with the deal."

"It better not." Dante fights his tone under control and tries to switch back to talking casually. He waves at me. "This is Saul's daughter, Melody."

Niko doesn't look at me, either. He holds out his hand to shake mine and mumbles, "Nice to meet you."

I say the same thing and we both face front. I don't want to have anything to do with anyone who screwed over my father in business.

My father going into business with Niko a second time sounds like a terrible idea.

My father speaks very highly of Dante Helme. My father wouldn't be doing this at all if he didn't want to do a deal with Dante.

Niko excuses himself. "I'm gonna go mingle. I'll talk to you gentlemen later. We can iron out the details then."

He wanders off and the tension fades.

"Are you crazy?!" my father hisses as soon as he leaves. "Why the hell did you have to invite him in on this deal?!"

"I already told you," Dante returns with plenty of his old iron. "He runs the biggest trucking network in the country and he's also the best. Besides, I know him and I trust him."

"Well, I don't!" my father snarls. "I will never trust him ever again! How can I trust him with funds from this deal? He won't trust *me* with funds, either! It won't work without a joint account where we can make purchases and take in cash from sales. How do you plan to do that when neither he nor I will agree to it?"

"You'll have to agree to it."

"Well, I won't! Give me one reason why I should. I could put my money in there and never see it again! He could cut me off at the knees—which is exactly what he did last time!"

Dante frowns at him and then his eyebrows shoot up. "There is a way you could do it—a way he would never be able to remove all access to the account."

My father groans and throws up his hands. "I don't even want to know! God only knows why I'm even considering this!"

"You're considering this because you need this deal and you want to work with me. All you have to do is arrange for Melody here to marry Niko."

I gasp out loud. "What?! I am not marrying him! Are you insane?! I'm already engaged to someone else! He's......he's a total stranger."

"It would be a legal fiction—just for the purpose of this deal," Dante tells me. "You would be married in name only—but it would give you unlimited access to the funds in the joint bank account we plan to use for the deal. Even if Niko tried something, you could get the money back."

My father passes his hand across his eyes. "This is outrageous."

"You can't do this, Daddy!" I practically shriek. "You already gave Taylor your blessing! You can't go back on that! I won't marry him! I *can't* marry him! No way! Forget it! You can't do this to me against my will."

Dante only shrugs, says, "Just think about it," and walks off into the crowd.

I round on my father. "You can NOT be seriously considering this, Daddy! I won't let you! I won't go through with it! You can't make me! I'm marrying Taylor! I don't even know this Niko guy!"

He wrings his hands. My stomach drops when I see him quivering in despair and looking everywhere but at me. "I have to, sweetheart!" he moans. "I need this deal like he says. I have to do it—and he's right. Niko is the only way this deal works."

"You're making me part of a business deal?!!" I practically shriek. "You can't do this to me, Daddy!!"

"If you don't do this, I'll be ruined. I might as well sell this house and forget about doing business in New York ever again. I bet everything on this deal. You'll just have to cut it off with Taylor for the good of our family."

I stare at him in horror, and right then, at the worst possible time, Taylor comes back carrying two champagne glasses.

I can't face him. I can't even be in the same room with him when my father explains this—however my father is going to explain this to Taylor.

I break away and run from the room. This is the worst night of my life.

Chapter 2: Niko

I stare up at Dante Helme in abject horror. I can't speak above a whisper. "You....what?"

"It's the only way you can both put funds into the joint bank account to do this deal. Saul doesn't trust you any more than you trust him."

"You're damn right I don't trust him!" I snarl. "The son of a bitch screwed me over on a deal and robbed me blind of millions. How the hell am I supposed to trust him ever again?"

Dante actually smiles at me. "That's interesting. He says exactly the same thing about you."

"Of course he does! He would say anything to weasel out of taking the blame. He's a toad. He's a conniving....."

Dante holds up his hand. "That's enough. I'm not going to listen to you two insult each other."

My brother Raymond comes over to us. "So you want Niko to marry the fool's daughter? How does that help us?"

"It gives both of you unlimited access to the bank account in question. It will be like a marital bank account, so Niko and Melody will always have access to the funds no matter what. If Saul screws over Niko, Niko will be able to get that money back. If Niko screws over Saul, Saul will be able to get that money back through Melody."

"Unless one of us transfers the money to another account," I growl. "Which is exactly what she would do to help her father screw me over."

"Melody is a sweet girl who doesn't have a dishonest bone in her body," Dante counters. "I've known her since she was a kid."

I snort at him. "She's a Gottlieb. Every bone in her body is dishonest."

He holds up both hands. "You're doing this or the deal is off. That's my final word."

He walks out of my office. I stare after him fuming in rage.

"We don't need this deal," Raymond remarks from the other side of the room. "We can pull the plug. Saddling yourself with a wife is the last thing you need right now—or ever."

I sink into the chair behind my desk and let my head fall back against the black leather. "I don't need the deal, but I do need him. I need to get on good terms with him so we can do business again later. If he's right about this deal, it could make us a ton of money."

"So you can share it with her when she cuts your nuts off? You're dreaming."

I compress my lips. I don't want to believe that my brother is right. I wasn't planning on getting married—not now, maybe not even ever.

My phone buzzes in my pocket just then. I pull it out and find a whole stack of paperwork from Dante.

It's all related to the deal—and everything related to the joint business bank account has Melody Gottlieb's name on it—right next to mine, Saul's, and Dante's

I groan in agony and cover my eyes. "No! Please God no!"

Ray looks at the email over my shoulder. "Damn! The guy isn't taking no for an answer."

"I can't believe Saul is going along with this. He must be either desperate or he needs Dante as much as I do."

Ray stands back with his hands on his hips. "You know, there may be a way we can turn this around."

"Please tell me," I mumble. "Please tell me you know a way we can turn this into a positive."

"Maybe this is the way you've been looking for all this time to get back at her old man. You could use this deal to screw him over for real—exactly the way he screwed you over."

"I can't," I growl. "Dante would turn against me."

"I bet you could figure out a way to do it that didn't have anything to do with business. You'll be living under the same roof with Saul's daughter—his beautiful, rich, sought-after daughter. This could be the perfect way to twist the knife where it counts. We can use her against Saul, steal his fortune, and take control of his part of the deal for ourselves. Dante never has to find out. He'll think Saul failed and Dante will be grateful to you for stepping into the breach to save the day ."

I don't answer. I don't want to think the words, *twist the knife,* in the same thought with any woman.

I distract myself by going through the emails. Everything else from the deal looks airtight.

Melody's name on everything is the only problem I can see with it. Dante really knows his stuff. That's why I want to do business with him.

Dante also sends over an appointment scheduled for tomorrow morning. The meeting is for me to meet with him and Saul to discuss every detail of the deal—and I mean *every* detail—including Melody.

I can already see how that's going to go.

I distract myself with every other detail of the deal besides that. I have enough to worry about running the rest of my business empire. I don't think about anything until the next morning.

I'm sitting in the back of the limo on my way to the meeting when Ray brings me back to reality. "So.....have you set a date yet?"

I glare at him. "This isn't a joke. If you treat it as one, I'm going to have to put my boot up your ass to make you shut up."

He bites back a smirk. "She is hot. You have to give her that much."

"Hot doesn't enter the equation."

"It does for everyone else. I saw Giovanni Nowaczyk hitting on her at Saul's gala."

"Did you also see Taylor Erwin driving Giovanni away? She's already engaged to someone else. They announced their engagement last year and Saul was right there in the middle of all the publicity events. He must have given Taylor the nod."

"A year? They've been engaged for a year and haven't tied the knot yet? I wonder why."

"What the hell difference does it make why?" I snap. "She's promised to another man. If she goes through with this, she'll do it hating me and counting down the seconds before she can tactfully get out of it."

"You'll be doing the same thing, won't you? So you'll both be in the same boat. Marry her, do the deal, and divorce her. I'm sure plenty of guys from the club have countless divorces under the belts."

I snort and look out the window. "I wasn't planning on becoming one of them. Divorce is the most expensive liability known to man."

"Then don't divorce her. Just keep her in the lifestyle to which she has become accustomed. You're already a monk. So you'll be a married monk with a wife you never see. How is that different from the way you live now?"

I don't answer him. I don't want a wife at all. I'm perfectly happy being married to my business. I don't have time to think about anything else—or any desire to.

I really wish the limo would just keep driving around in circles all day, but it pulls up at the venue pretty soon.

The venue for this meeting is on neutral territory in the conference room at Citicorp Bank building downtown—so Dante, Saul, and I are all on equal footing here.

Dante should have been the one to host me and Saul, but I understand why Dante wants to stay out of the middle. He basically already is in the middle.

He's the one insisting on this fake marriage. If anyone else suggested it or even put the screws on me and Saul to go through would this, I would suspect them of foul play.

I can't suspect Dante. He's too straight up. I've known him for years. I can't remember him doing anyone dirty in all that time.

No one ever accuses him of doing them dirty, either. No one ever accused me, either—not until Saul Gottlieb came along.

I could almost get on board with ruining him for that, but then I would be no better than he says I am.

I would also not be worthy to be in the same room with Dante. I'm only walking into the same room with him with a business deal on the table because he knows me well enough to not believe Saul's accusations.

Dante must be putting the same screws on Saul, but that doesn't stop me and Saul from glaring at each other across the room.

Melody isn't here, thank Heaven. I couldn't stand that.

I already know she hates me—probably as much as I hate her. I hate that she's the vehicle that got me into this situation.

It probably isn't her fault, but I can't help but resent her for it. I resent her only slightly less that I stew in fury at her father.

I don't feel the same fury toward Dante for some reason. I understand why he's doing this—and he believes in Melody for some odd reason.

His opinion means a lot. Asher Gottlieb is a raving idiot and an obnoxious asshole. I wouldn't trust him with a single dollar of my money.

Dante and I agree about him, but Dante says she doesn't have a dishonest bone in her body.

I don't want to believe that about anyone with the name Gottlieb, but I guess I have no choice but to go through with this.

Asher stands behind his father. Asher doesn't glare at me or Ray. Asher is too stupid to read the room and pick up the palpable hostility radiating back and forth.

Dante waves at the big table in the middle of the room. "Sit down, gentlemen. Let's all shake hands and commit ourselves to making this deal as good as it can be. You can lay your grievances to rest and you never have to see each other once we ink this deal."

Ray and I approach the table on our side. Saul and Asher approach from the other side. Dante stands at the head of the table.

Neither Saul nor I extend our hands at first. I don't want to be the one to do it first, but when Saul still doesn't move, Dante clears his throat loudly and I stick out my hand.

Ray and I shake with Saul and Asher. Asher actually has the nerve to grin at us like the moron he is. I can't believe I'm actually sitting down at any conference table with him.

At least his name isn't on the deal. I can always insist that he doesn't get involved—or I can just refuse to deal with him. If he calls me to arrange any detail of this deal, I can tell him I won't talk to anyone whose name isn't on the paperwork.

That's bound to piss him off. Good. I hope it does.

Dante says, "Sit down, gentlemen," and we all sit down. He sits at the head of the table because...well, he's Dante.

He pulls out his phone and starts going over all the paperwork he sent me yesterday. He asks me and Saul questions about the arrangement.

Saul plans to bring in the goods from overseas. Dante owns the marketplace outlets, both online and brick-and-mortar.

My job is fulfillment—trucking, warehousing, and delivery. It's the perfect system—as long as each of us handles our end.

I'm not worried about my end. Dante's side of the equation is solid, too.

I find myself studying Saul in more detail when Dante asks Saul about the whole importation process.

If I'm right about Saul being in trouble, then he might not have the money to bring in these goods. He might have to buy them on credit.

That would be irretrievably stupid, but at least it won't affect me or Dante if it all snaps back to bite Saul in the ass. The goods will already be paid for.

Dante is obviously thinking the same thing. He questions Saul extra closely about his finances. I'm surprised Dante doesn't ask to see Saul's books.

I sure as hell wouldn't want to see Saul Gottlieb's books. They should be turned over to the IRS as far as I'm concerned—but I digress.

Dante finally puts his phone down on the table. "Now let's talk about this business of Niko and Melody getting married."

I stiffen to my chair and clench my jaw to stop myself from saying what I really think about that.

"I still don't think this is necessary, Dante," Saul mutters.

"Really?" Dante counters. "You sounded pretty certain at the gala that you wouldn't be willing to introduce funds into the same bank account that Niko had access to. You agreed then that this marriage is the only way both of you can feel secure to mix funds." He turns to me. "Are you willing to go through with this marriage so we can get this deal off the ground?"

I nod down at the tabletop. I don't trust myself to say a word.

"That leaves you, Saul." Dante's voice cuts like a knife. "Make a decision right now. If you decide to back out on the deal, we can all walk away and start looking for something more deserving of our time. If you decide to go through with this, we need to start planning how to introduce Niko and Melody to the public. We need to get the ball rolling so it works in our favor as a marketing angle for the deal."

I stop breathing waiting to hear Saul's decision. Please dear God in Heaven, let Saul back out of this! Then I can withdraw with my dignity intact and maybe do a deal with Dante and another supplier.

I'm really glad Melody isn't in the room to hear Dante talking about working her wedding as a marketing angle. I can just imagine what she'll say if Saul tells her that's what this is.

She must have already figured it out by now.

My blood runs cold when Saul casts his eyes down at the table in front of him. "I already promised Taylor Erwin," Saul mumbles. "I have to break my promise to him."

"That's your decision," Dante counters. "What you do with Taylor and how or if you keep your word to him is your own business. Are you in or are you out?"

Saul heaves a broken sigh. "Yeah...I'm in."

"Good, then we can start making plans." Dante picks up his phone, but those words stab me in the guts. Saul is going through with it—which means I have to go through with it.

I will never back out on a deal with Dante Helme. Hell no.

"I think you should hold another gala, Saul," Dante goes on. "You can introduce Niko and Melody and announce the date of their wedding—which means we have to decide on a date. When do you two think would be best?"

Saul shrugs. He still won't look up. "I guess it doesn't really matter in the end—as long as we make a good showing. We can pay extra to get everything done right away as long as it looks good."

Dante turns to me. He talks to Saul harshly, but Dante's eyes soften when he looks at me. Maybe, just maybe he understands what he's asking.

"What about it?" he asks me. "When do you want to do it?"

"As soon as possible," I tell him. "I just want to get it over with so we can all concentrate on more important things."

Saul's head shoots up. "Watch your mouth, you piece of trash! That's my daughter you're talking about!"

I turn on him baring my teeth. I held back before. I'm not going to sit here and let him insult me.

"I don't want to marry her at all," I snarl. "Take her back if you feel that way."

"Stop it!" Dante snaps. "What about the eighth of next month, Niko? Will that work for you?"

I glance over at Ray and he nods. "That will work," I reply. "Just tell me what I gotta do and I'll be there."

"Does the eighth work for you, Saul?

Saul only shrugs. He's back to looking defeated. "Fine," he mumbles. "Whatever."

"I don't want to hear whatever," Dante snaps. "You're the father of the bride, so you're responsible for the wedding and you better make it a good one. You better go all out on the dress, the flowers, the decorations, the cake—everything. Make it convincing—and make the gala a big deal, too. Niko—I understand how you feel about this, but you better make it convincing, too. I expect you to pull this off and make everyone believe that you and Melody are madly, rapturously in love."

Asher and Ray both laugh. I am going to have to kick Ray's ass as soon as we get back to our own office building.

Neither Saul nor Dante laughs. Dante glares at Asher and Ray harshly enough to shut them up.

"Don't worry about me," I growl. "No one will know any different."

"Then that's settled. I'm setting a date for the twenty-seventh of this month for all of us to get together with our lawyers and ink the deal. Make sure you both go over all the paperwork and bring up any issues or changes you want to make before then."

We all stand up. I go through the motions of shaking hands with Saul and Asher.

Dante pulls me into a hug when he shakes my hand. This deal better be worth the nightmare I'm going through to make it happen.

He reads my mind and his eyes soften again. "Keep your chin up. Everything will work out."

"It better," I mutter.

He only smiles at me and turns away to shake hands with Saul. Dante doesn't hug Saul. Their handshake comes across as stiff, formal, and awkward.

My one consolation in this is that Dante isn't nearly as warm with Saul as Dante is with me.

"I expect you to email me about all the wedding preparations," Dante tells him. "I want to make sure everything fits our brand and that it's up to standard for the media blitz."

Saul only nods. "I understand. I'll keep you informed. I'm sure Melody will want to get started on the preparations right away."

I turn to the door to leave. I'm sure Melody will want to get started on the wedding preparations right away, too. The wedding is only three weeks away. That doesn't leave much time.

Chapter 3: Melody

"You did what?!" I bellow.

"I had no choice!" my father yells back. "This was when Dante set the date! I had nothing to do with it!"

"The eighth of next month is in three weeks, Daddy! You couldn't get him to push it back—like at least another month?!"

"No, I couldn't! We all agreed we had to get it done as soon as possible!"

"Well, how in the name of God am I supposed to plan an entire wedding in three weeks?!" I demand. "It's impossible!"

"It isn't impossible! It will just cost more—a lot more! We'll have to tell the caterers, florists, and decorators to expedite the whole thing."

"You said you were doing this deal because you were on the ropes financially! You made it out like you would be ruined if you didn't do this deal!"

"I will be!" he roars. "Is that what you want to hear—that I'm on my last legs?!"

"Then how the hell can you afford to expedite what could be the biggest wedding this year?! Where are you getting the money for this!"

"That's my business—not yours! How I pay for it doesn't concern you!"

"I'm going through with this for you, Daddy—because you said you needed this deal to survive! You better believe it concerns me!"

"We don't have time for this!" he snaps. "Just start planning it—and make it a good one because the press will all be there watching—and you and Niko better make it convincing. Everything depends on it."

I snort and throw up my hands to spin away from him. He's completely unreasonable. He won't budge on this whole wedding disaster.

He turns away, too, and comes face to face with Taylor. He sits on a bench against the side wall of our living room.

Taylor has been sitting there listening to me and my father argue about this ever since my father came home from his meeting with Niko and Dante.

Taylor doesn't get involved in the fight. Does Taylor even realize that my father is breaking our engagement so he can marry me to some idiot I don't even know?

My father's demeanor changes completely when he faces Taylor. My father's features sag and he lowers his voice to a broken croak.

"I'm sorry, son," my father quavers. "I hate what this is doing to you."

Taylor stands up. "Don't worry about it, Sir. It's only temporary, right—and it isn't like Niko and Melody are ever going to do anything. This whole marriage is just a legal fiction so you can do the deal. As soon as it's over, they can dissolve the marriage and Melody will be all mine."

My father tries to smile and fails. He winds up grimacing instead. "Yeah," he husks. "Exactly." He looks back and forth between me and Taylor. "I guess I'll leave you two alone."

He walks out of the room. I sink onto one of the couches, bury my face in my hands, and groan. "I can't believe this is happening to me!"

Taylor sits down next to me. "Don't get too disheartened about it. It's just a loophole so Niko and your father can use the same bank account. It doesn't mean a thing."

I look up at him. "I'm sure glad you see it that way. I would be more concerned about offending you than anything else."

He smiles down into my eyes and kisses me. "I love you and I'm going to marry you. No business deal is going to come between us. I promise you that."

I fall into his arms and shut my eyes in the safety of his presence. I don't want to be anywhere but right here with him.

I hold onto his words with all my might. It's only temporary. This marriage is just a legal fiction. It isn't like Niko and I will ever do anything.

As soon as he and my father conclude this deal, we'll dissolve the marriage. Then Taylor and I will be together forever.

He pushes me up straight and gets a wild glint in his eyes when he kisses me. "Hey, we might even be together before the deal ends. You and Niko can live apart. Then you and I can be together as much as we want."

"But I want to marry you!" I tell him. "I don't want you to be some dirty little secret."

He laughs, leans in, and kisses me hard enough to push me back on the couch. "Come on. I can be your dirty little secret—your extra dirty little secret...."

He dives in and starts kissing me much harder, He plunges his hand between my legs and I squeal when he starts rubbing me.

He muffles the sound with his mouth on mine. He drives his tongue into my mouth and I reel off into a delirious orgasm when he rubs me through my pants.

I give myself into his hands. He's the man of my dreams. I don't want anyone else.

He finally eases off enough to let me sit up, but he won't stop kissing me for anything. "You're all mine," he murmurs into my mouth between kisses. "Your heart and soul are mine. No one can take you away from me."

I look down at the slip of paper in my hand with all the wedding preparations listed on it. "Can't we just run away together?"

He laughs again. "You wouldn't do that if it could leave your father ruined."

I cover my eyes again. "Don't remind me."

"If he's right, then he stands to make enough money to put him back on top. Who are we to argue if it takes a little legal gymnastics to get there?"

I heave a sigh of my own. "I guess so."

He kisses the side of my head and stands up. "You better get started with the preparations—and have some fun with it. Think of it as theater. You can go completely over the top and make it as big, beautiful, and extravagant as you want to. No one can blame you—and it doesn't mean a thing. Just enjoy yourself. Don't think about anything else. I'll see you later."

He leaves me sitting there staring at the list.

I don't want to plan any wedding unless I'm going to be marrying him, but I have no choice. It looks like I really am going to go through with this.

Chapter 4: Niko

"**A**re you sure you really have to do this?" Ray murmurs in my ear.

"We've already gone over this a thousand times," I counter. "I can't back out now—not after we already signed the contract."

He stops me in the foyer of Saul Gottlieb's giant ballroom. Ray grimaces at the luxurious surroundings. They don't mean anything to either of us anymore.

"I know we signed a contract and you think the sun shines out of Dante Helme's ass, but Jesus, man! Getting married?!" he winces. "Damn! You're letting the whole team down."

"There is no team, sonny." I pull the jacket of my tux down and straighten my sleeves. "I wouldn't care about shafting Saul, but I couldn't do that to Dante. He's a member of The Billionaires' Club. None of them would do business with me again if I bailed on Dante, now that we have a signed contract."

Ray makes a few more faces. I see him winding up to say more about how I'm on my way to my own funeral by getting married.

I can't let him pour any more doubts into my head. "I'm doing it, so don't question it again," I tell him. "I need you backing me up, not making me question my decision."

I don't give him a chance to answer. I sidestep around him and walk into the ballroom.

This is completely different from the last time I came here. I'm here as Saul's guest—the guest of honor, in fact. I'm officially engaged to his daughter even though I never proposed to her.

This gala is the first of many press pushes to spread the word that Saul and I are best buddies now.

I can see the minute I spot him that there is still no love lost between us. Him becoming my doting father-in-law and me becoming his devoted son-in-law doesn't change a thing between us.

Melody is the only unknown quantity in all of this. I don't see her anywhere in the ballroom—not yet.

She has to make a grand entrance so the press all pays attention to how beautiful and stylish she looks.

All the decorations, food, and pageantry of this gala are supposed to broadcast to the world how rich the Gottliebs are—and how rich Melody and I are going to be after our union joins the Gottlieb fortune with mine.

These reporters sure must be gullible. Not one of them actually checks Saul's books to find out if he really is as rich as everyone says he is.

He isn't. He wouldn't do business with me at all if he didn't need this deal. He wouldn't sell out his only daughter unless he absolutely had to.

I might pity him for that if he hadn't shafted me in our last deal. Now I only hope this deal breaks him the way he deserves to be broken. I hope this deal takes him down and finishes him forever.

The final blow won't come from me. I can just sit back and enjoy watching karma bite him in the ass the way I know it will.

His own incompetence will destroy him. Then he won't be my problem anymore.

Melody will be my problem, but I won't be the first guy in The Billionaires' Club to go through a divorce. I'll just have to do it quickly to minimize the damage.

I've spent the last week picking Judah Hayes's brain about how he set up the trust to protect his assets from his psycho ex. I have to scramble to do all of that before the wedding.

Fortunately, my business is all incorporated. Most of it is already protected—all except my shares in it.

Reporters shove their microphones into my face as soon as I walk into the ballroom.

"Niko!" one woman reporter calls out. "How did you keep your romance with Melody a secret all this time?"

I pretend to grin at her. "I don't kiss and tell. That's between me and Melody."

"Did you have a problem with Taylor Erwin?" some guy asks. "Did he get jealous when you stole Melody from him?"

"You would have to ask Taylor that," I reply over my shoulder. "I don't know and I don't care what Taylor's reaction was."

"How come we never heard about Melody and Taylor breaking up?" another woman asks. "She was happily engaged to Taylor for a year and then, overnight, we got the announcement that you were engaged to her."

"I just told you I don't know anything about what happened between Taylor and Melody."

"Didn't you know if they broke up before you started seeing Melody?" the same guy asks. "Did you start seeing her while they were still together?"

I turn all the way around to confront the reporters. I don't want to have to explain any of this to anyone. I definitely don't want to lie about it.

I'll be lying at the altar when I vow to love, honor, and cherish Melody until death do we part. Like hell.

Fortunately for my sanity, a commotion breaks out on the other side of the ballroom. All the reporters turn to face the other end of the room.

They all rotate their cameras and video equipment up to the high balcony above the ballroom floor. The reporters snap a million pictures and yell out to get Melody's attention.

She steps into view wearing a beautiful off-the-shoulder white gown. It runs straight down her sides and hugs a perfect hourglass figure.

She looks stunning below the neck. Her push-up top gives her a stacked, voluptuous appearance that would knock any man off his feet.

She looks stunning above the neck, too, to be totally honest. Her dark hair tumbles across her ivory shoulders in glistening brown waves. Her soft brown eyes reflect the glow of all the chandeliers hanging level with the balcony.

She looks every inch the society bride that she is. She looks good enough to step off the red carpet or anywhere else alongside the most beautiful and celebrated women in the world.

I can't see any of that when I look at her. She's my enemy. Her beauty, grace, and appeal only make me hate her even more.

She's nothing but another Gottlieb. She's a branch from Saul's tree. I don't need to know anything else to hate her guts.

Her eyes lock on me from that distance. I would have to be blind not to see that she hates me just as much.

The reporters keep flashing their cameras while she and I study each other from that distance. The reporters probably think we're exchanging a romantic gaze of knowing soul connection. Little do they know the truth.

This position would be the perfect angle for me to admire how incredible she looks. I would definitely find her attractive—but only if I knew nothing else about her.

The moment only lasts a few seconds before she shakes it off, turns aside, and bursts into a huge, beaming smile. She smiles for the reporters and they take even more pictures of her smiling at them.

Her smile looks genuine. It doesn't have the fake, painted-on look of some celebrity smiles. Is it possible she really is happy about this?

Her brother Asher appears out of nowhere and escorts her down the stairs to the ballroom floor. The reporters surround her all yelling the same questions.

Everyone wants to know how Melody and I supposedly got together and carried on some whirlwind romance without anyone finding out.

Everyone wants to know how she stopped being engaged to Taylor Erwin and wound up engaged to me instead. I don't have any answers for that. How is she answering those questions?

She glides her way across the ballroom coming closer to me. I dread the moment when she gets near me.

Then I'll have to smile for the cameras, too. I'll have to pretend that I'm happy about all of this and that I couldn't be happier and prouder to have Melody Gottlieb on my arm.

She takes extra long migrating through the crowd. She answers each person's question and smiles just as brightly at each person.

All my doubts about her attitude toward me go straight out the window when she finally looks up at me. Her eyes go hard and a brick wall slams into place between us, but she doesn't stop smiling.

She crosses to my side, rises on her tiptoes to kiss me on the cheek, slips her hand into my arm, and turns outward to face the press. I smile, but no way am I doing as good a job of making it look genuine.

The reporters snap even more photos of me and Melody together. It's a good thing I can't see anyone with all the flashes blinding me.

Saul and Asher come over to us. They stand on either side of me and Melody.

In the last cruel twist of irony, Saul stands on my end of the line, puts his arm around my shoulders, and we all smile at the cameras. The happy family that wasn't.

Chapter 5: Niko

The mob of reporters comes over asking me, Melody, Saul, and Asher Gottlieb even more questions about how it all went down. Too many people are asking me questions. I have no trouble avoiding the ones I don't want to answer.

Then come the questions about me and Saul going into business together—supposedly to secure our family legacy for the next generation that Melody and I are going to spawn. I have to stop myself from laughing at that.

The press push goes on a lot longer than I expect it to. As soon as a few reporters finish mobbing us, new people move in to take their places. This could go on all night.

I'm still standing there drowning in noise when Saul's security team moves in. They shove the reporters away and herd everyone out of the ballroom.

Saul waves Melody and me away toward the buffet and the drinks table. "Come on over and get some refreshments," he tells us. "We have another press spot in an hour. You can relax until then."

Melody keeps her hand on my arm. I face front no matter what. I don't even look at her to check her reaction to any of this. I'm sure she's smiling as brilliantly as ever.

I can't smile anymore. I might be able to once the next raft of reporters comes in, but not now.

The caterers try to give me something to eat, but I'm not hungry. I don't trust myself to drink—not when I'm swimming with the sharks like this.

Dante finds us, shakes hands all around, and talks to Saul about the other spots on our press circuit. If Dante sees how stiff Melody and I are acting toward each other, he doesn't show it.

I can't even say we're acting stiff toward each other. We both pretend the other isn't there. I would be able to delude myself completely if not for her hand resting on my arm.

Saul eventually leads us into a private room behind the ballroom. Plush couches and armchairs line the three walls opposite the door. A carved wooden coffee table sits in front of them.

"You two can take some quiet time by yourselves in here until ten o'clock," he tells us. "That's when the next press push starts. We'll deal with everyone else until then."

He leaves me and Melody alone. I don't want to sit down. I don't want to let my guard down at all.

She slips her hand out of my elbow, gasps slightly, and runs her hand across her forehead. She does it carefully so she doesn't mess up her hair or makeup.

"Jesus! How much more of this do we have to go through?" she mutters under her breath.

Those words make me glance up at her. Just for a fraction of a second, I make the mistake of thinking maybe she and I could connect over the fact that neither of us wants this.

Her beautiful features twist into a mask of pure venomous hatred when she sees me looking at her. "What the hell do you want?" she snaps. "Don't start getting any ideas about this. I'm doing this for my father. You're nothing to me."

I snort at her. "Do you honestly think I would come within a hundred miles of you if I didn't stand to make some decent money off of this deal? No one wants you, sweetheart. Trust me. You can sneak out and bang Taylor in the broom closet every damn night for all I care. I wouldn't touch you with a ten-foot pole. I would just as soon not look at you at all."

She curls her upper lip back and bares her teeth at me. "And you think you're some kind of prize? Is that it?"

I nod. "I know I am. I can walk out there and get any girl I want. If Erwin wants you, that just goes to show what a bitch he is."

Her mouth falls open and she gasps in horror. "How dare you?!"

"I just can't figure out whether he's your bitch or your father's. Maybe he's both. Either way, you're welcome to him. I hope I never see either of you again after this—so you go on and act as noble as you want. You're doing it for your father. I'm doing it for the money—just so we're clear on everything. You're a piece of coin to everyone involved in this deal. I hope you're happy."

I turn aside just to make my point. I don't care if I hurt her feelings. I hope I do.

She must think a lot of herself if she really believes I would get ideas about her. Never in a million years would I touch anything with the name Gottlieb attached to it.

I expect her to gasp in horror again. I really hope she understands just how worthless she is—to everyone. Her own father is selling her on the auction block to line his pocket.

Now I know for a fact that Saul Gottlieb is totally without honor and integrity. He has no shame, no standards, no boundaries, and no scruples about anything—not even his own family.

Instead, she snarls under her breath through gritted teeth. "You son of a bitch! I swear I'll take you down for that."

I barely glance at her, but once I see her narrowing her eyes in pure murderous fury, I don't let myself look away. "Your father is going to come out of this penniless and ruined. You mark my words. You're the vehicle that will make that happen. I don't have to do anything. You're the one who will destroy everything your father holds dear. I just want you to hear it from me first."

She glares at me with steam billowing out of her ears until the door opens and her father returns. "The reporters are just coming in now," Saul tells us. "It's time."

Neither Melody nor I move for a second. I really don't want to go out there and smile for even more cameras, but I'm the one who signed my name on the dotted line for this.

She slips her hand into my elbow again, throws back her head, and we both walk out onto the ballroom floor.

We meet another tide of reporters all snapping pictures and firing off exactly the same questions. They drown each other out so Melody and I don't have to explain anything.

The reporters also take pictures of us with Saul and Asher. Don't ask me how Ray stays out of the limelight. Asher is here, so Ray should be here.

The hostility radiating off of Melody becomes palpable the longer this goes on. She definitely hates me—as if I wasn't quite sure.

How much does she understand about her father's business standing? Does she realize by now how close he's running to the wind?

Why else would she agree to this? She said she's doing it for her father. She must realize that he'll crash and burn without this deal.

He'll crash and burn even with the deal. She probably thinks I'll screw Saul over and that's what will bring Saul down.

She doesn't understand his business well enough to realize his own stupid mistakes will cost him everything. I just need to make sure the same thing doesn't happen to me while he's at it.

I finally get out of the ballroom. Ray and I climb into the limo on the way back to our penthouse building. He lives in the penthouse just below mine.

I collapse on the seat and groan. "How much more of this do I have to put up with?"

He chuckles and checks his phone. "Two more galas and a slew of press conferences before the wedding."

I throw my arm over my eyes. "Great."

"Sit up, open your eyes, and listen to me. I figured out a way we can sabotage the deal, steal the Gottliebs' goods, and drive Saul into insolvency."

"We don't have to do anything," I reply. "He's paying for all his goods on credit. He won't be able to service that debt. Then his part of the deal will fall through."

"That's what I'm saying. We can bypass him and purchase the same goods from his supplier, now that we have his name on this deal. We can sell the goods separately through another marketplace."

I take my arm down to scowl at him. "We would screw over Dante if we did that."

Ray bursts into a mischievous grin. "I know! That's what's so great about this deal. We would corner all three pieces of the puzzle. We would purchase supplies, sell through another marketplace, and we would still control fulfillment. We don't need these two."

I put my arm back over my face. "That won't work. We couldn't do Dante dirty like that."

"What is your thing about Dante?" Ray counters. "This is business. Anything goes."

"You're wrong. He's a member of The Billionaires' Club....."

"You say that like he's some kind of sacred cow and we aren't allowed to compete with him."

"This is not competition. This is shafting a good man and using his contacts and influence to castrate him and leave him with nothing. I'm not going to do that to someone in the club. I won't even do it to Saul."

Ray makes another face. "You're going soft in your old age."

"Saul will do himself in. We don't have to try. Dante is too good to mess with like that. Just leave the deal alone. If it goes the way I think it will, Dante and I will be doing business with Saul's suppliers pretty soon anyway—without Saul involved."

Ray shakes his head and looks out the window. "I don't know about you sometimes."

"You don't have to know about me. I'm the one in charge of this business, not you. Leave the deal alone."

He doesn't answer and he doesn't look at me. I can't figure out why he's so set on ruining this deal. Saul Gottlieb never did anything to Ray.

"If you really want to help me, make sure I'm legally insulated from this arranged marriage," I tell him. "That's what I really need right now—nothing else."

He grimaces again, but he won't make eye contact. "That's the whole point of this marriage—to stop you from being fully insulated. Once you let the bitch in, she'll have access to everything, including all your assets that aren't included in the deal."

Now it's my turn to glare at him. "Don't ever let me hear you calling her that—not ever again. Are we clear on that?"

He snorts and looks away. "Don't tell me you have a thing for her now."

"I hate her as much as you do. That doesn't mean we're going to start calling her names—either to her face or behind her back. She doesn't want this, either. Don't call her that. That's my final word."

He goes silent and stares out the window at the streetlights passing the limo.

Ray knows me too well not to understand exactly what I mean. He won't badmouth Melody—not like that.

We can both hate her for being Saul's daughter. That doesn't mean we have to get disrespectful about it.

I don't blame her for hating me. If anything, that's the only thing I respect about her.

Chapter 6: Niko

I walk into The Billionaires' Club and spot Jackson Metcalfe, Judah Hayes, Dante, and Kevin Drake standing together near the buffet.

I don't want to deal with anyone else, so I walk straight toward them.

Kevin holds out his hand to me. "I hear congratulations are in order."

I shake his hand. "If you want to call it that."

"How did you make Taylor Erwin disappear so fast?" Jackson asks. "I haven't seen a single reporter try to interview him about your engagement."

"I guess the guy knows when to make himself invisible." I pretend to look around. Giovanni is laughing with two other members near the pool table.

Rory Kahn stands not far away watching them. Rory knows better than to get involved in anything Giovanni finds funny.

I've been meaning to ask Kevin to investigate Giovanni's womanizing. If Peirce Robbins could screw around with Judah's wife on club premises while club meetings were going on, what is there to stop Giovanni from doing the same thing?

He'll bang anything that walks. He has definitely hit on plenty of married and engaged women. That never stopped him.

I would never bring a woman I was serious about around him. He's too volatile.

My mind switches to Melody before I can stop myself. I'm not serious about her. I'm not in a relationship with her. I'm not even interested in her.

This is a legal mechanism. It will never be anything more than that.

I catch Dante watching me to make sure I hold up my end of the performance. None of these guys will be able to spot a chink in my armor.

I never talked about girls in front of them before. I'm not going to start now. They all know I'm engaged and about to marry Melody Gottlieb. I don't need to go into the gory details.

Jackson and Judah start talking about one of Jackson's ongoing deals. Everything the guy does interests me. It interests all of us.

We all turn to listen to him, but right then, Asher Gottlieb rolls in. His presence casts a chill over me.

His presence casts a chill over everyone. He's technically a billionaire because of his ownership share in his father's assets. He technically qualifies for club membership, but no one wants to accept him.

Kevin wipes his face of all expression, murmurs, "Will you gentlemen please excuse me?" and goes over there to intercept Asher before he does too much damage.

He smiles way too broadly at everyone who doesn't want him here—including me. He wouldn't be here at all if not for his father.

Kevin can't turn Asher away as long as he qualifies for membership and abides by the club rules and guidelines. Asher might be an insufferable social clod, but he hasn't done anything yet that could get him banned.

I don't want him here, but his membership status isn't my decision. I already hate Saul. I can hate Asher from a distance in the same way. I don't have to deal with him.

He strides around the room shaking hands with everyone, talking way too loudly, and gushing on at the mouth like every man here is his best friend.

He blasts his way through our group. He shakes my hand for a split second and doesn't wait long enough even for me to say a word before he moves on to Jackson, Judah, and Dante.

Asher is such a moron that he doesn't treat Dante any differently than Asher treats any old schmo off the street.

Any decent businessman would take extra time to re-establish the connection with Dante—if Asher ever even had a connection with Dante.

Asher is too thick to realize how important Dante is to him. If I was in Asher's position, I would spend almost my entire visit to the club talking to three people—me, Dante, and Kevin.

Kevin is our membership officer. He's responsible for orienting new people who join the club.

Kevin's goodwill will be instrumental in determining if Asher fits in with us or gets thrown out on his ass for breaking the rules.

Asher obviously doesn't understand that. He's too spoiled and self-centered to realize how important it is for him to maintain his existing business relationships—namely his established relationships with me and Dante.

I don't even care when Asher moves on to the next group. I don't want to talk to him anyway. I don't want to have to put in the effort to hide how much I can't stand the prick.

I'm fully ready to go back to our much more interesting conversation about Jackson's latest conquests.

Asher's loud voice interrupts us again. "So what are we ironing out today?" He brays with loud laughter at the joke he supposedly just made.

No one else laughs. I catch sight of Rory narrowing his eyes at Asher. He sure knows how to turn people against him. It's one of the very few things he knows how to do and he does it well. That doesn't bode well for his future business prospects.

He naturally migrates to Giovanni's group. Giovanni is just shallow enough to put up with Asher's abrasive personality. Giovanni doesn't care who he talks to as long as whoever it is thinks he's God's gift to humanity.

He and Asher should get along well. I don't know about Asher's exploits with women, but Giovanni may have found a kindred spirit there.

I turn my back on both of them. I sure hope they hit it off. Then the rest of us won't have to deal with either of them.

Kevin watches Asher from afar. Kevin makes sure Asher doesn't get into any further trouble with the members. Then Kevin returns to our group.

"I guess he'll be all right for now," Kevin murmurs.

"The keyword being, 'for now'," Judah adds. "Give him a few days to put his foot in it."

Jackson turns to me. "What is it like doing business with him?"

"I'm not doing business with him. I would never do business with him. I'm not even doing business with his father. I'm doing business with Dante—no one else."

"You're doing business with Melody, aren't you?" Kevin asks.

"No, I'm not." I try to keep my voice smooth and casual. "I'm doing business with Dante there, too. Dante is the only person in the whole transaction that I am doing business with." I cast a glance over my shoulder toward Asher. "I don't trust that fool as far as I can kick him. I would never trust him with anything."

That seems to drive the nail into any discussion of Asher Gottlieb or anything else related to my deal with Dante.

I have to remind myself of that every minute of the day. I'm doing business with Dante Helme. He's the only person in the deal that I would ever do business with.

I notice him watching me extra closely. I don't care that he heard me criticize Asher in front of the other club members. I would do a lot worse.

I'm not the only man here who criticizes Asher. No one wants him around—unless it's an ego-driven narcissist like Giovanni. They're perfect for each other.

The configuration of our groups changes pretty soon. Rory comes over to talk to us and then Jackson and Judah go to the buffet to get something to eat.

Kevin and Rory wind up talking about something related to the club admin. They're both officers in the club, so they have plenty to talk about.

Dante sidles over to me. "How's it going, champ? Are you getting the pre-wedding jitters?"

"Of course not because I'm hardly getting married. This is all a farce for the cameras."

"And for the legal protections," he points out. "Don't forget that's the reason you agreed to this, remember?"

"I'm not convinced the legal protections really outweigh the legal risks. I have to protect myself from being married. I'm not sure anymore if it's even worth it."

"It's too late to back out now. We have a contract in place."

"I know and I fully intend to honor our contract. Just don't ask me to be happy or excited or thrilled about this."

He smiles at me. "I don't expect you to be, but you do have to deal with Saul. You have to be civil to him and treat him like the business partner he is. You can't go around telling people you're only doing business with me."

"Well, I am only doing business with you. I can't stand the creep. I wouldn't be doing any of this if you weren't involved."

He starts to say, "I understand that, but....."

He breaks off when Saul Gottlieb walks into the club.

He looks around and smiles like Asher talking to Giovanni is the best thing that could ever happen. Maybe Saul hopes Giovanni's business sense will rub off on Asinine Asher.

Giovanni knows how to run a business. You can say whatever you want about his personal life. The guy knows how to handle money, business, and the marketplace. He's on top of his game and a titan in his industry even though he's still so young.

Saul doesn't interfere with Asher talking to Giovanni. That's mistake number one—or maybe it's mistake number five thousand four hundred and seventy-six in Saul's tarnished career.

If I had a son I was trying to teach about business, Giovanni is the last person on the planet I would ever let my son hang out with.

I would be too worried about my kid turning into a Giovanni clone. I would want the kid to develop some sense of self-respect—not to mention earning the respect of his peers—which Giovanni doesn't have.

That doesn't concern me, either. Nothing about Clan Gottlieb concerns me as long as they keep up their end of the deal.

Saul's expression turns black when he sees me and Dante standing next to each other.

I would expect Saul to avoid any contact with me, but instead, he sets his features in a mask of iron and comes straight toward us. This should be interesting.

Dante shakes Saul's hand. "How is it going?" Dante asks. "I didn't expect you to be here. I thought you had an incoming shipment for the warehouse."

"I did—and I do—but we have a problem." He turns his cold, hard eyes in my direction. "We have a problem."

I stiffen when I realize what he means. *We* have a problem—meaning he and I have a problem.

Great. I'm not even married to his spoiled brat of a daughter and he already has a problem with me. At least Dante is here to sink the brand for us.

I don't have to say a word. Dante does it for me. This is his baby. He can run interference. "What's the problem?" he asks.

"Niko here was supposed to send seven trucks to the docks to pick up the shipment. The trucks never showed up. The shipment is still sitting there on the boats waiting—and every hour it sits there costs me twenty thousand dollars in extra fees." Saul points at me. "That money is coming out of your pocket. You're breaching our contract."

I pull out my phone and tap on the app I use to track all my consignment and shipping transfers.

"The trucks did go to the docks." I show him and Dante the screen. "The trucks are still sitting there waiting to take on cargo." I frown at the numbers. "This says my drivers have been there for six hours overtime and the goods still haven't arrived."

"That's impossible!" Saul snaps. "There must be some mistake loading the numbers into the app."

"They should sync automatically." I switch over to the phone keypad. "I'll get to the bottom of this."

I dial the number for the shipping yard manager. I've done so many transactions through his yard. I'm on a first-name basis with the guy.

He answers right away and I put the phone on speaker so Saul and Dante can both hear. "Yello!" the manager answers.

"Hey—Mick! It's Niko Holloway."

"Hey, bro!" Mick replies. "What's the word, thunderbird?"

"The app says seven of my trucks are sitting at your yard waiting to take on cargo. The app says the shipment hasn't come in. The importer says the goods are there and my trucks aren't. I need you to confirm which it is."

"Yeah, man. Your trucks are here. Your drivers keep coming into my office demanding answers."

"So where are the goods? The importer says the ships are all in dock waiting to offload."

"The ships are here. The goods aren't."

My eyes shoot up. Saul stares at me with huge eyes. "What do you mean—the goods aren't there?"

"The ships are empty. They came all this way carrying nothing. There's nothing for your trucks to load on. You better contact the supplier and find out what went wrong. It could just have been a computer error on the supplier's end."

I gulp. "Yeah, man. Thank you. I really appreciate your help."

I hang up and make a strategic decision not to say, *I told you so,* to Saul.

He blinks at me with huge, dull eyes before he turns away shaking in nervous agitation. I don't say a word. I don't have to. All three of us know what this means.

I can't ship goods that didn't arrive on the ships. Dante can't sell goods that didn't arrive on the ships.

I shudder when I realize what happened. The ships sailed all the way from the other side of the world. They must have been empty when they left. They made the trip without any cargo at all.

All of that expense will land on Saul. He won't recover a penny of this.

If someone at the supplier messed up, he'll have to pay for shipping a second time to bring the goods over for sale. Will this be the straw that breaks him forever?

Chapter 7: Melody

I stand in front of my bedroom dresser mirror and study my reflection. I'm wearing the biggest, fanciest, most expensive wedding dress that money can buy.

I look like a bride—but I don't feel like one. I look like a completely different person than the Melody I know so well.

I'm betraying Taylor by marrying someone else, but I'm betraying myself more than anyone else. I try again and again to trick myself into believing I'll see him at the church when I show up at the altar.

I trick myself into believing that I'll be saying, *I do,* to Taylor instead of some scumbag who wants to destroy my father.

Asher's voice startles me from outside my bedroom door. "Are you ready, sweetie? The limo is waiting to take you to the church."

I tear myself away from the mirror. It only raises more questions than it answers.

I open the door. Asher breezes right in, hugs me, and puts his arm around my shoulder. "You look outstanding. You're going to be so perfect out there."

I groan. "Tell me again why I agreed to this."

"You agreed to go through with this because no one in the world would believe I was actually serious enough to marry someone."

I snort. I can't even take comfort in my own brother's misfortune.

He's right. No one takes him seriously—probably because he doesn't take himself seriously. He treats everything as a joke—especially my father's business.

Asher is supposed to take over the father's empire after my father passes on. I don't see that happening. I don't think anyone else does, either.

I don't want to spend my wedding day thinking about Asher and his problems.

He kisses the side of my head. "Do you want me to walk you down the aisle?'

"You can't. Daddy is walking me down the aisle."

"Oh, right. I forgot." He laughs at his own joke. "Well, do you want me to escort you with a loaded shotgun to drive the Holloway boys away from you? Niko might be a Terminator, but Ray is a slimeball."

"Look who's talking." I pick up my skirts and head for the door. "I better go."

He accompanies me downstairs to the limo, holds my hand to help me get in, and then gets in behind me to ride with me to the church.

Asher is wearing an immaculate tailored black tux, but not even that can make him look respectable. He would look sloppy in anything.

He kisses me on the forehead at the church entrance. "Congratulations, sweetheart," he murmurs. "You're doing the best thing for the family."

I don't answer. I don't want anyone to congratulate me on any of this. This is the worst day of my life.

I don't pay any attention to the bridesmaids and their escorts filing up the aisle to take their places by the altar.

Niko stands up there with his back to the church. At least I can explain that by tradition. He doesn't turn around when the music changes.

His brother Ray smiles at me over Niko's shoulder. I even hear Ray whispering in Niko's ear.

What is Ray saying to Niko right now—that there's still time to back out of this wedding and that I'm too frumpy for a stud like Niko?

Is Ray telling Niko that the two of them will destroy my father and me along with him? I wouldn't be surprised.

My father comes toward me. I become aware that he looks sloppy, too. His tux doesn't make him look any neater than Asher. They're two peas in a pod of different ages.

Niko and Ray always dress immaculately. They always look outstanding with every detail in place, even when they're conducting their day-to-day business.

I can't see Niko from the front right now. I don't have to. I can see every meticulous detail of his clothes and grooming from here.

I try to shake that off. I wouldn't trade my family for anything—especially not anything as shallow as a man's appearance.

My father offers me his arm and we head down the aisle. Niko still doesn't turn around.

I concentrate on the back of his head. That's the only way I can keep my focus and my nerve to go through with this.

He actually kind of looks like Taylor as long as he doesn't turn around.

I hope everyone takes my lack of emotional reaction as a combination of nerves and determination. I don't want anyone to realize how much I really don't want to go through with this.

I stop next to Niko. He glances over at me for the first time and his eyes go steely hard before he faces front.

That one look sends a shiver up my spine. Wow. He really hates me. I didn't realize until this moment that he harbored that much resentment over it.

I hate him, too. I hate him for putting me in this position—except that he didn't.

Does he even comprehend that I'm not the one who put *him* in this position? Does he realize that I don't want to be in this situation, either?

I just have to keep going. The priest starts reciting the service. I barely feel it when Niko and I extend our hands and the priest wraps the embroidered cloth around our wrists to bind us together.

I'm marrying Taylor. I'm saying, *I do,* to Taylor. This is Taylor standing next to me right now. I'm in love with Taylor. I'm going to spend the rest of my life with Taylor.

Niko's own words weasel into my brain at that moment.

You can sneak out and bang Taylor in the broom closet every damn night for all I care. I wouldn't touch you with a ten-foot pole. I would just as soon not look at you at all.

Taylor and I will never be legitimate—not as long as I'm legally married to Niko.

My heart and soul revolts against this. I can't go through with it, but I have to. My father and my whole extended family stand behind me watching me promise myself to a man I hate.

Niko doesn't radiate hostility the way he did at the gala. I don't feel anything from him. He doesn't react to anything except to respond when the priest reads the vows.

We finally turn to face each other. Niko's eyes go dead when he slips the ring on my finger. My whole body feels numb.

I say the words, *I do,* but I feel nothing. Those words mean nothing. All of this might as well not even be happening.

Niko's expression only comes to life when the priest says, "I now pronounce you man and wife. You may kiss the bride."

Niko takes a step toward me and locks onto me with full, unwavering eye contact when he raises my veil. His eyes tell me in no uncertain terms that none of this means anything to him, either.

He holds my gaze just long enough to send me a clear message. He's about to kiss me, but that's all part of the act. He feels nothing for me and I feel nothing for him.

He sweeps his arm behind my back and pulls me against him in a masterful, powerful move that makes my heart stop. He's stronger and more self-possessed than I gave him credit for.

He holds me there against him for a split second—just long enough to drive his message home. He's the one in charge here. He's doing this because it serves him.

He isn't smitten with me. He doesn't feel in the least bit slighted or wronged that I don't like him. He doesn't want me to like him.

He dives in and kisses me hard. He doesn't just give me a peck and pull away. He stays there crushing my mouth under his. No one seeing him would ever guess he didn't mean it.

He tears away just as fast and stands there holding eye contact and holding me tight against his body.

His muscles vibrate with high tension. He doesn't back away from feeling me against him or letting me feel myself against him.

His eyes challenge me in ways no one ever has. He wants me to feel that. He doesn't care at all if I reject him. He rejects me as much or more.

He decides who he gets involved with, how, and why. This business deal doesn't change his feelings for me. Nothing can ever change that.

He finally lowers his arm, takes my hand, and bursts into a full smile when he turns me to face the crowd.

Rice showers over us. The moment shatters and he pulls me back up the aisle toward the church exit.

Chapter 8:
Melody

Niko pulls open the door of a long, sleek, black limo parked in front of the church. It isn't the same limo that brought me here just a few minutes ago.

He steers me into the seat, dives in after me, and slams the door. All the wedding guests yell, wave, take pictures, and throw rice until the limo pulls away from the curb.

Niko collapses back on the seat and shakes the rice out of his hair. "Phew! That's over with!"

I look away. He couldn't make it more obvious that he doesn't want to do any of this.

I was the one who originally said I didn't want to have anything to do with him. Now I feel the sting every time he makes one of those comments.

I feel the sting every time he *doesn't* make one of those comments. He does it with his eyes. He's rejecting me and pushing me away.

No guy has ever rejected me before. I realize that only now—now when I'm sitting in the limo with him.

I'm married to him—the one guy in the world who doesn't want me.

Every other guy I've ever dealt with wanted me for my father's money. I didn't let myself believe that until now.

Taylor didn't come after me for my father's money. I was the one who initiated things with him. I was the one who asked him out. I was the one who kept our conversation going in the early days.

Our relationship developed over time—but what if he wanted my father's money, too? What if he was never interested in me for anything else? What if that's the reason he never asked me out?

Niko puts me completely out of his mind, now that the wedding is over. We still have to get through the reception and a few other press spots. Then......

His phone rings in his pocket. He takes it out. He doesn't even excuse himself when he answers it. "Yeah," he clips. "Yeah, we're in the limo on our way to the reception. Yeah, I know. Okay. I'll see you t here."

He hangs up and starts tapping on the screen. Is he checking his emails?

He spends a long time tapping out a block of text. Is he answering emails or texts? What the hell did I get myself into?

He doesn't even look at me until the limo pulls up in front of the reception venue. It's in the ballroom of a luxury hotel downtown.

Niko only looks up from his phone to squint through the window at the hotel building. He puts his phone back into his pocket, gets out first, and offers me his hand to help me get out.

Reporters pack the sidewalk between the limo and the hotel lobby. Security guards hold back the crowd.

Niko escorts me inside. He smiles and waves to all the cameras. His smile looks genuine, but I know better.

Cheers break out when we walk into the reception. The guests whistle and surround us to hug us, shake our hands, and congratulate us.

I have to smile at everyone, but this whole thing makes me sick.

Asher comes over, hugs me, and congratulates me, too. Why? He already knows how I feel about this marriage of convenience.

Then Niko's brother Ray comes over. He hugs me, kisses me on the cheek, and squeezes my hand when he congratulates me.

Is he trying to send me a message, too? Ray must understand how Niko feels about me. Ray is Niko's righthand man. They run Niko's companies together.

So why are Ray and Asher both acting like this marriage is real? Are the two brothers just putting on an act for the cameras, too?

I could believe that about Ray, but not Asher. Asher even acted that way when we were alone together in private. Why?

Niko and I have to stand there holding hands and receiving everyone's well wishes. My face starts to ache from holding this fake smile for so long.

My hand is also getting cramped and sweaty from holding Niko's. He has thick muscular hands that dwarf mine even though he isn't that much taller than I am.

He feels me trying to adjust my grip. He loosens his just enough and then clasps it again. Neither of us can move even if we want to.

We both wind up facing away from each other. At least I don't have to look at him.

The time finally, finally comes when we can sit down at the tables and eat the wedding meal. My father and Asher sit on my side. Ray sits on Niko's side, so neither of us has to talk to each other.

My father and Asher talk about business. I pretend to listen so no one will assume I should talk to Niko.

I can only guess that Niko and Ray are also talking about business. I should probably pretend to be interested in Niko's work, but I can't bring myself even to face in his direction.

Then comes the time when everyone makes toasts. My father gives an incredibly fake speech about what a good businessman Niko is and how admired he is in the business world. That much is true, at least.

My father also goes on at length about how proud he is to have Niko as a son-in-law, how in love Niko and I are, and how certain my father is that Niko and I will be happy together.

I have to force myself to smile up at my father. No force on God's green Earth can force me to shed tears over this.

A bunch of other people give toasts, including Ray. He's Niko's best man. Ray also spins the crowd a big story about how Niko and I met, how it was love at first sight, how Ray knew from that very first night that Niko had found the one, and it was all downhill from there.

Ray blabs just as long as my father about how awesome I am, how happy I make Niko, and how Ray knows that Niko and I are going to go the distance together.

Ray waxes poetic in the same way about how thrilled he is that Niko found the love of his life and how Ray already considers me a sister and I'm part of their family in ways he never thought possible. He raises a toast to me and my continued happiness in marital bliss with his brother.

I tune out the rest of the toasts. Then we have to cut the cake.

Niko gives me another hard, direct stare of challenge when we both take hold of the knife to cut the cake. We're playing an act here—a charade.

At least we don't have to dance. I dance with my father and then it's time for me and Niko to leave.

I throw the bouquet. I don't even look to see who gets it. It's someone I don't even know. It might even be one of the reporters. That would be just perfect.

Niko and I wave to everyone and run off to the limo before it drives off into town. We're spending the month of our honeymoon in the Mandarin Oriental Hotel.

I find myself shrinking to get farther away from him the closer we get to the hotel. He better not expect anything from me when we get there.

He takes my hand again when we get out of the limo, but he lets go immediately once we get into the elevator. He takes the room key out of his pocket and uses his arm to hold the elevator open for me when we get out on the right floor.

I keep a safe distance between us while he unlocks the door. He pushes the door open and stands back to let me enter first.

I don't move. I stay where I am and wait for him to go first.

He turns around and frowns at me. "What are you doing? Go inside."

"So you can do something to me on the way? Forget it. You go first."

He snorts and storms into the room. It's an enormous suite with a series of palatial living rooms, multiple bedrooms, and views over Central Park.

He takes the key with him and lets the door swing shut behind him. He doesn't stop to check that I enter behind him.

I have to leap forward to catch the door before it locks me out. He would probably leave me standing in the hall in my wedding dress. He wouldn't even open the door to let me go inside.

He's in the act of throwing the room key card, his regular keys, his phone, and some other stuff on the side table by the door. He doesn't look up when I walk in.

Actually he does look up because I skirt him in a wide arc to get past him. I don't want to go anywhere near him.

Once I get clear, I cross the main living room. My suitcases stand next to the couch.

He turns aside from the table and walks into the living room, too. I sidestep again. "What are you doing?!" I snap. "Stay the hell away from me!"

"What is your problem?" he counters. "I was going to look at the view. Do you think I give a shit about you or what you do?"

"Do you think I'm stupid?! You went to all this trouble to marry me. Do you think I don't know what that means? I know how to defend myself. I'll put you in the hospital if you come near me."

He glares at me through narrowed eyes for a second. "You actually think....I would dirty myself....with *you*?! You're delusional." He walks straight past me, throws himself down on the couch, picks up the remote controller for the enormous flat-screen TV, and turns it on.

My attitude infuriates me. Dirty himself? He didn't actually say that about me.

"You bastard!" I snarl. "I wouldn't come within a hundred miles of you if I had any choice about it."

"Oh, you had a choice about it," he clips out the side of his mouth. "No one held a gun to your head."

"No, you held a gun to my father's head—which is just as bad. Do you think I don't know what you did to him? He's in trouble now because of you! You might as well have held a gun to *my* head!"

His head snaps around and his eyes flash with deadly fire when he skewers me to the bone. He raises himself slowly off the couch and stands there seething in front of me.

"I.....did...to him...?!" he hisses under his breath. "You think.....he's in trouble.....because of me?!"

"Don't think I don't know! He told me all about it! You screwed him over....."

He overreacts so fast he scares me. "He screwed *me* over!" he roars. "He reneged on a contract and cost me millions when I was just starting out in business! He destroyed me! I had to start over from nothing! *He* was the one who screwed *me* over! Your father is in trouble right now because he's a rotten, corrupt, incompetent criminal who keeps fucking up everything he touches! He'll do the same thing with this deal! Dante and I can only afford to deal with him because we've taken so many precautions to protect ourselves! Don't you get that?! You're a precaution I have to take to protect myself from *him*—not the other way around! *He's* the one who would take *my* money! He's the only party in this deal who needs the money bad enough to steal it!"

"YOU SON OF A BITCH!!" I shriek. "Don't you dare talk about my father like that!"

"I'll say whatever the hell I want about the jackass, now that we're behind closed doors. Your father already tried to shaft me in this deal through his own moronic incompetence. Dante was standing right there and heard the whole thing. Your father is in debt up to his eyeballs! You marrying me can't save him! Nothing can! He'll wind up in the gutter where he belongs!"

"I HATE YOU!!" I don't even know what else to say to him. I don't know enough about my father's business to disprove anything Niko says.

What if he's right? What if my father is the one who did all of this? What if Niko is the one doing my father an enormous favor by going through with this?

I can't think that. I can never think that—not about this fiend standing in front of me.

"YOU BASTARD, I HATE YOU!! I NEVER ASKED FOR ANY OF THIS! I NEVER WANTED THIS!!"

"And you think I did?! Do you think I can't get a woman whenever I want one? I don't need you! You need me." He throws himself back down on the couch and picks up the remote. "I would rather cut my arm off than touch you. I would rather gouge out my eyes than even look at you. You go do whatever you're going to do and leave me the hell alone. I have better things to do."

He flips a few channels on the TV. He's serious. Watching some stupid trash on TV is more important to him than I am.

Why do I even care? I don't want Niko Holloway looking at me anyway.

The way he says it cuts me to the quick. What if he's right about all of this? What if I'm nothing but a pawn in a giant game of Pass-the-Buck?

I'm not even that. I'm nothing more than a piece of ass my father sold to further his business interests. My own father treated me like a prostitute.

I'm lucky Niko doesn't actually want me. I'm lucky he at least has the decency not to see me that way.

I turn away to go back to my suitcases, but being in the same room with him hurts too much. I try to stop my lips from quivering, but the tears in my eyes blur the suitcase. I can't unzip it.

I rush into the nearest bedroom and barricade myself in the enormous bathroom. I'm still wearing my wedding dress—the wedding dress that means nothing.

I can't even change out of it into my normal clothes. All my clothes are in my suitcases. I would have to go back to the living room.

Niko would ignore me if I went in there. He would keep watching TV and doing things on his phone. He really does have better things to do than have anything to do with me. I'm the last thing on his mind.

I would almost rather have him hate me than completely put me on a shelf like this. I can't stand this.

I sink down on the floor in the corner, cover my face, and let the sobs out. No one can help me. Now I'm trapped here with this psychopath for a whole month.

I can't leave or the press might suspect that the wedding was a sham. I have to keep up appearances to give the deal the best chance of succeeding.

I'm doing this to help my father. If I'm not doing that, then there's no reason for me to do it at all.

Chapter 9: Niko

I turn up the volume on the TV so I don't have to hear Melody crying in the bathroom. I still know she's in there. I don't have to hear her.

I kick myself for saying the things I said to her even though they were all true. She isn't responsible for any of this.

She's the victim of her dirtbag father. She's caught in a shitty situation the same way I am—except that it's somehow so much worse for her.

I fume on the couch and switch the channels a few more times, but I'm too irate to watch TV.

She actually thought I would attack her and force myself on her—as if I would do that to any woman. I wouldn't do it to my worst enemy—which she definitely isn't.

I hate her father—and I hate her for representing him. Now I can't get rid of him because I'm stuck with her.

I can feel sorry for myself until the cows come home. What I'm going through is nowhere near as bad as what she's going through.

Her father promised her to a man she loved. They were engaged to get married.

Then her wretch of a father broke his word and sold her down the river to someone she doesn't even know—someone her father taught her to hate. That has to hurt.

I finally switch off the TV. I can't concentrate with her crying in the other room.

I might be the last person in the world she wants to see right now. In fact, I'm certain I am, but I have to do something.

I go into the kitchen, make a roast beef sandwich, pour some potato chips on the plate next to the sandwich, and add a few candies from the dish on the coffee table.

Then I pour some tropical juice into a glass and carry the plate and glass into the bedroom. She left the door open.

She didn't leave the door open to the bathroom. I would have to be deaf not to hear her sobbing in the corner.

She sits on the floor behind the door. Poor kid. She must be really broken up about this.

It must hurt even worse to finally hear the truth about her father. He probably spun her a big story about how I was the one who screwed him over and left him penniless.

I don't knock before I go into the bathroom. I don't want to give her the option to tell me to go away.

I won't go away. I can't. She just has to deal with me the same way I have to deal with her.

I walk in, shut the door behind me, sit down on the floor next to her, and put the plate and glass in front of her. "Are you hungry or thirsty?" I ask. "I know you just ate at the wedding, but sometimes crying can make you hungry and dehydrated. At least drink some juice."

I'm trying to act my nicest toward her, but she only breaks down sobbing even harder. She howls in misery.

I don't know what will help her, but I wouldn't leave a total stranger in this kind of agony. I put my arm around her shoulder and hug her.

She falls against me bawling her eyes out. I don't even have to ask why. She is the only person who really got shafted in this deal.

I wait a long time before she slows down enough to sit up straight. She crumbles again when she sees the food and juice I brought her, but she sobs silently.

Snot starts to run down her upper lip. I grab the toilet paper roll and hand it to her so she can blow her nose.

I wait some more until she slumps in resigned depression.

"Listen," I murmur. "We're both stuck in this with no way to get out of it—not for a long time. You hate me and I hate you, so let's just try to make the best of it without destroying each other. Okay?"

Her features screw up in another wave of brutal agony. She nods down at the crumpled tissues in her hand.

"I would never force you to do something you don't want to do and we aren't here for that anyway," I go on. "You never have to worry about me. If you want me to stay away from you, I will, but I don't want you to be afraid to be in the same room with me. I wouldn't do that to anyone. You have no reason to be scared of me."

Her voice cracks with sobs. "Thank you!" She chokes on her own tears. "I don't know what's happening to me! My life is in the gutter—and I don't even know why! I don't know how any of this happened!"

"It happened because you were trying to help your father. Listen. You don't have to sit in here on the floor. This is crazy. I'll bring in your suitcase and you can change your clothes. Then you bring your food and juice out to the living room. We can spend the evening watching a movie or something. Okay? Forget all this honeymoon stuff. It doesn't mean anything."

She nods down at her hands again. She keeps twisting her tissue again and again. It's so damp that it shreds in her hands.

"Here. Drink some juice. You need it." I place the glass in her hands, wait just long enough to see her take a gulp, and let myself out of the bathroom.

I don't care what happens as long as we can spend the next month being civil to each other. I'm going to be trapped here with her. I don't want to spend the time fighting and yelling at each other.

I wheel her suitcases into the bedroom and find her standing up in the bathroom. She's blowing her nose again and started to pull the bobby pins out of her veil. At least she's doing something.

I leave her there, shut the bedroom door, go back to the kitchen, and make a second sandwich for myself. I'm just sitting down on the couch to eat it when she comes out.

She's wearing a pair of huge, quadruple oversized, extremely fuzzy pink pajamas with hearts all over them. I can't help but laugh when I see her. "Nice! That looks cozy."

She grimaces when she puts her plate and half-empty juice glass down on the coffee table. "This is my escaping-from-reality outfit."

"It's perfect. I wish I had one. I need to escape from reality quite often, in fact."

"Stop it," she mutters and sits down on the couch.

She sits down at a safe distance, but at least she doesn't sit all the way over jammed into the opposite corner of the couch.

She sits in a normal position as if she was sitting next to her brother or a platonic friend.

I take a bite of my sandwich and pick up the remote. "So what do you want to watch?"

"What are the options?" She picks up one of her candies, twists off the wrapper, and puts the candy in her mouth. "Don't make it anything meaningful or tragic."

I pick up the laminated streaming guide from the other side of the coffee table. "We have *Home Alone*....."

She practically chokes on her candy. "Seriously?"

"Or we could watch *The Blues Brothers, Austin Powers, Raising Arizona*......"

"*Raising Arizona*," she interrupts. "No contest."

I look up. "Really? You like it?"

"I love it. I've already seen it at least twenty times. That's the one."

"Okay. That was easy." I put the guide down, navigate to the streaming service, and switch on the movie.

The opening titles start playing and she giggles to herself even before the all-too-familiar song ends. "Thank you for this," she tells me. "I really needed this."

"Of course. There's some ice cream in the freezer if you really want to drown your sorrows."

She grimaces at me again. "Let's not take this too far."

I laugh again. This movie is going to be just what the doctor ordered.

The movie itself starts rolling and she starts reciting every single line of dialogue. She has the whole damn movie committed to memory.

I would normally find that irritating if I was trying to watch a movie. I can't resent her for it. She obviously needs this a hell of a lot more than I do.

I've already seen the movie multiple times myself. I don't need to hear what's going on and I'm enjoying watching her more than the movie.

She laughs herself silly at the funny parts. She gets wistful when Hi and Ed find out they can't have children of their own, but Melody still smiles through those parts, too.

The movie finally ends. She sinks back on the cushions with a sigh when I switch off the TV. "That was great," she breathes. "I love that movie."

"Do you feel better now?" I ask. "Are you sure you don't need ice cream?"

She actually smiles at me now. "I'm fine. Thank you again. I think I better get some sleep. I'll see you later."

"Good night."

She goes off to the same bedroom and shuts the door. Good. She really is a reasonable person after all.

I should have realized that before. I shouldn't have gone off on her, but I suppose I needed that, too.

I just need to direct my anger where it really belongs. That isn't her.

Chapter 10: Niko

I wake up the morning after the wedding, take a shower, and put on my suit for work. I don't need to pretend that this honeymoon thing is real. I have a business to run.

I go out into the living room and see Melody's bedroom door still closed. I hope she's getting plenty of sleep in there.

I don't want to disturb her, so I leave without making breakfast, get myself a latte and a bagel on the corner, and head for the office.

I walk in to find Ray standing behind my desk. This is nothing unusual.

"Hey, Casanova!" he teases. "Did you make her toes curl in ecstasy last night?"

I compress my lips in annoyance and push him out of the way so I can sit down in my chair. I look at the screen he was just looking at on my computer. "What are you working on?"

"I was just going over the numbers from Saul's last shipment that wasn't." He bumps my shoulder. "Come on. Spill the tea. What is she like? Is she a screamer?" He changes his voice to a high-pitched squeal. "Oh, Niko! You're so big and strong and hard and manly! Oh yes! Oh yes! Oh yes!"

"Shut the hell up before I slap you," I mutter. "Get your head out of the gutter and pay attention to business."

He won't stop grinning at me. I really hate him when he acts like this.

I really could punch his face in for talking like that about Melody—as if this deal isn't bad enough for her as it is.

I try to take my mind off it by reading the spreadsheet on the screen. The deal is coming together nicely.

"The numbers from that missed shipment are throwing all the other numbers off, but apart from that, Saul's imports are all showing gains once they make their way through the system."

"Don't you want to check the joint bank account?" Ray asks. "The one you're supposed to be sharing with that hot wife of yours?"

I ignore the reference. "What about it? Why would there be any problem with it?"

"Your profits from this deal go into the joint account before they get transferred to your personal bank account. Don't you want to check that someone on the Gottlieb side isn't siphoning off the funds before they get to you?"

I don't want him pouring poison in my ear when this deal is only getting started, but his words raise my suspicions.

I log into the joint account I share with Melody. Saul's funds go in there, too. They get deposited under her name and then transferred to one of Saul's operating accounts.

I go through every transaction one after the other, but I don't find anything fishy here. Everything looks above board, but that doesn't set my mind at ease.

I check my calendar. "We have a meeting with Murdoch and Sons later today to sign the papers on my assets trust. I need to step up my efforts to insulate my assets from anyone in the deal getting their hands on anything."

"What about Dante?" Ray asks. "You worship the ground the guy walks on. Are you trying to insulate yourself from him, too?"

"I'm insulating myself from everyone. I don't worship the ground anyone walks on enough to let them screw me over. This marriage is bad enough. Who knows what else could go wrong?"

I get a call on my phone right then. The call is from my executive assistant, Emory. His office is right outside mine where he can run interference on anyone I don't want to see.

"Is something wrong?" I ask. "Why are you calling me at this time of the morning?"

"You aren't going to believe this," he murmurs under his breath. "You have a visitor. He wants to see you."

"Who is it?" I ask.

"It's Asher Gottlieb," Emory whispers. "He says he wants to talk to you about the business deal between you and his father."

I frown to myself. "He showed up here unannounced and wants to see me? Are you serious?"

"Yes, Sir," Emory breathes. "He actually tried to blow smoke in my eyes and tell me he had an appointment to meet with you. When I said he didn't, he said I must have made a mistake and suggested that you get yourself another EA."

I snort. "Okay, man. I'm hanging up now."

"What do you want me to do with him?"

"Send him in. I'll find out what he wants."

He snorts. "You're a braver man than I am."

I have to laugh and we hang up.

"What's going on?" Ray asks.

"Asher Gottlieb is here."

Ray raises his eyebrows. "Really? That's odd."

"I don't think there is another word that describes him better. He obviously wants something from us."

"You mean he wants something from you." Ray retreats to the other side of the office, throws himself down on the couch, and hangs his arm over the back. "I just have to see this."

I relax in my chair. I won't be getting any work done until I find out what the hell is so all-fired important that Asher Gottlieb would land in my office unannounced first thing in the morning on a work-day—and then lie to Emory about having an appointment.

I knew Asher was shady. I just didn't know he was this shady. Something tells me this meeting is going to be much more informative for me than it will be for him.

I get a sudden brainwave, take out my phone, and switch on the voice recorder app to record our conversation. I might need this as evidence later.....for something.

He breezes in grinning like the fool he is. He walks around with that dopey grin plastered across his face like he's the greatest thing since sliced bread.

I stand up to shake hands with him and immediately sit down. I don't invite him to sit down, but he does it without waiting for me to say it first.

He glances across the office at Ray watching from the sidelines. I'm suddenly glad I have a chaperone for this meeting.

Asher sprawls in the chair with his legs spread and both arms hanging over the sides. He doesn't even have the good sense to sit up straight.

"This is unexpected," I begin. "What can I do for you?"

"My father and I have some questions about your trucking operation. We want to get some more detail on how you're storing and fulfilling orders that go through Dante's retail outlets."

I stop myself from frowning. "What do you want to know? The investor's prospectus on our website includes more information than you could possibly want. All you have to do is read that. I won't be able to tell you anything that isn't already in it."

"We've already gone over all of that. We have more detailed questions."

"Like what?" I ask.

"We want to know how involved you are with day-to-day operations."

"I'm not involved in day-to-day operations—not at all. I have a whole hierarchy of managers who handle that."

"The reason I ask is because you seemed very involved when we had that mishap with the shipment that didn't come through. You could pull up all the information at the press of a button—and you got the dockyard manager on the phone within the first few rings. You found out exactly what you wanted to know without jumping through any hoops—and you didn't assign any of your management people to find out for you."

Now I really do frown. "Yeah? So? That's what running a business is. I solve problems the managers can't solve."

"So you don't think the managers could solve that?"

I take a second to study him across my desk. Now I know something weird is going on.

For a start, he wasn't even present during my phone call to Mick or when I checked the shipping information on the app.

Saul was the one who complained about the shipment not going out. Asher was across the room making stupid high school locker room jokes with Giovanni at the time.

How did Asher find out about it? He could only have found out from Saul.

My mind goes through a bunch of wacky contortions imagining Asher hacking the security camera footage from the Billionaires' Club. That doesn't make nearly as much sense as Saul talking about it after the fact.

That begs the question. Why is Asher asking me about it now?

I choose my next words with care. "I didn't have to get one of the managers to solve it because your father brought the problem straight to me. I made a phone call to someone I knew. That solved the problem. It would have taken more time and complicated matters if I sent your father through the managers when he was already standing right in front of me."

Asher nods like he knew that all along. Who the hell does this idiot think he is?

He pulls out his phone. "What is the app that you used to track the trucks that were supposed to pick up the shipment? I want to see how the app works."

"It's an internal app we use within the company. You won't be able to see it."

I stop myself from saying anything else—like asking why the hell he wants to track my trucks, shipments, pickups, and deliveries.

He's up to no good. I don't know what he's doing, but it will definitely work against me.

Should I tell Dante about this? Are Asher and Saul pulling the same crap on Dante?

I have to correct myself. I don't believe Saul is behind this. He might be a terrible businessman who doesn't know one end of his books from the other. He might even be criminal in his practices.

If he is, he's criminally negligent. He isn't outright nefarious. He's too naïve for that. He's too naïve even to realize what he doesn't know about his own business operations.

I can't say the same for Asher. The guy doesn't have much business experience—not in real time.

He is corrupt enough to be outright nefarious. He would have to be if he wants to see my operations app. No one has to draw me a map on that.

He's so completely out of it on appropriate professional behavior that he doesn't even think twice before he asks, "Is there any other way I could check out your operations?"

I take a second to decide what to say. "Why exactly do you want to see them? Is there something about my operation or anything about the way I'm fulfilling my end of this deal that concerns you? Is that why you want to see it?"

"No, not at all. I'm just curious."

Bingo. So that proves it. Saul isn't involved in this at all. This is one hundred percent Asher. He's the one doing this on his own initiative.

"How about this?" I tell him. "I'll arrange for one of my people to give you a tour of our operations depot. Then you'll be able to see it for yourself. I know the perfect person to show you around. He can answer all your questions about how our operation works."

His face falls right in front of me. He can't just come right out and say he wants to monitor my trucks, deliveries, shipments, and pickups. That would be a breach of our code of confidentiality.

Asher already knows this. He already knows he can't ask that and he doesn't. I would have him dead to rights if he did.

He has no choice but to agree to the tour. He won't be able to get any specific information on individual shipments—which is obviously what he's fishing for.

I stand up to signal him to get the hell out of my office. He takes the hint and stands up to copy me.

He doesn't button his jacket when he stands up. He leaves it hanging open. Everything about him looks sloppy. He *is* sloppy. He's an idiot. He's just idiotic enough to be dangerous to everyone around him.

I make up my mind then and there to drive him out of The Billionaires' Club. I can't just come right out and insist that Kevin throws Asher out. That would be against the bylaws.

I'll have to warn everyone about him, though—starting with Dante. Everyone who might feel even slightly tempted to go into business with Asher needs to know ahead of time what he's capable of.

I escort him as far as the door and send him on his way. Then I call Emory and arrange for one of the depot managers to show Asher around.

I send down instructions that Asher shouldn't see anything confidential or even remotely important. I send instructions to keep the tour as superficial and meaningless as possible. That should keep the dope out of trouble.

I return to my computer, close every page I have open, and switch over to the internet. Ray stands up and paces around the room. "That was strange."

"It isn't strange. He's up to something. He's trying to end-run us. I just have to find out how before he actually does it."

Chapter 11: Melody

I sit cross-legged on the couch in the Mandarin Oriental honeymoon suite and pull one of the wedding gifts toward me.

I read the card. It's from a certain Mr. and Mrs. Ronald and Sabrina Hemmingsworth. I've never heard of them.

The box weighs a ton with a huge white satin bow on top. I don't want to mess up the bow, so I slide it off and take extra care pulling off the shiny gold and silver wrapping paper.

I open the box, unfold a bunch of layers of tissue paper, and take out an enormous cut Waterford glass sculpture of a swan. It's huge and weighs more than Fort Knox itself.

I put the sculpture on the coffee table. The sculpture must have cost a mint—just like all the rest of the gifts Niko and I received.

I feel bad about accepting these gifts for a wedding that didn't really happen, but I guess the people who sent them don't need to know that.

I pick up the next box. This one is much smaller, lighter, and has black and gold ribbon. The card reads, *Congratulates and all the best wishes for your happiness, Charles and Angelina Rothschild.* I don't know them, either.

I open the box and lay the ribbon and wrapping paper in the growing stack at my feet.

I unfold another nest of tissue paper and pull out a magnificent Fabergé egg. Golden curlicues surround the outer surface. The box includes a carved gold stand for the egg to rest on.

I put the egg on its stand next to the swan sculpture. The egg is so much smaller and less obtrusive, but it must have cost a lot more.

Whoever these Rothschilds are must be loaded—which explains why they wanted to get involved in my wedding.

I'll have plenty of time during this honeymoon to stare at the egg. I'll have to ask Niko which if any of these gifts he wants to keep.

He'll probably say he doesn't want any of them.

I got a completely different view of him last night. He was so kind when he didn't need to be.

He took care of me and helped me deal with all these conflicting feelings I'm struggling with. I'll always be grateful to him for that.

He even tolerated my stupid obsession with *Raising Arizona*. Niko didn't make fun of me or ridicule me for reciting the lines. He didn't interrupt me even once. He just let me do my thing so I could get over my upset about the wedding.

I actually believed him when he said he would never hurt me or make me do something I didn't want to do.

I don't know why, but I trust every word he says as the truth. He has no reason to lie.

That's what makes it so hard when he says these awful things about my father. I don't believe Niko would lie about it.

Some part of me does believe that my father would lie about it. He has all the reason in the world to lie about it.

He would want to make himself look like the injured party—especially if he's talking to me or someone in the business world. Of course he would never admit he did anything wrong.

Niko doesn't strike me as the kind who would do the same thing. He's too righteously infuriated over my father's actions.

My father is righteously infuriated over Niko's supposed actions, too. I can't explain why I believe Niko over my own father, but I do.

I pick up the next box. It's a medium-sized box somewhere between the swan sculpture and the egg.

I'm just about to read the card when I hear footsteps on the balcony outside. No one should be out there. The balcony is hundreds of feet off the ground and it's supposed to be private.

Whatever newlywed couple is staying in this suite should be able to do it out there on the balcony without anyone seeing them.

I don't plan to do it with anyone out there, but the balcony isn't connected to anything else. No one should be able to get there without going through the suite itself.

I put the box down and stand up to go see who it is when Taylor walks through the open balcony doors right in front of me.

"Taylor!" I exclaim. "What are you doing here?! You can't be here!"

"I had to see you!" He grabs me, pushes me back against the wall, and starts kissing me madly, deeply, and passionately.

I'm still wearing my I-hate-the-world pajamas. My hair is a mess and I haven't taken a shower this morning. I woke up to find Niko already gone, so why bother making myself presentable?

Taylor doesn't notice. He grabs me through my pajamas and crams his body in hard to pin me against the wall.

"I need you so bad!" he husks into my mouth. "I can't live without you! Come on. Run away with me! Let's go right now! You don't have to stay here."

"Hey!" I rip off his mouth and push him away hard enough to make him step back. "I can't leave! I'm already married! It's too late. I married Niko. You said you were okay with that."

"That was before! I can't stand to see you and him splashed all over the media. You should be with me—not him."

He attacks my mouth again, so I don't have a chance to explain again that I want to be with him instead of Niko.

Taylor rakes his hands down my sides, finds the waistband of my pajamas, and starts to weasel his hands down inside my panties. Is he going to take me right here against the wall of the honeymoon suite?

A loud beep and a click startle both of us into jumping apart. The apartment door opens and Niko breezes in.

He takes one look at Taylor and goes straight to the kitchen. Taylor and I stand frozen in shock while Niko opens the fridge, takes out a clear plastic box of cherries, and carries it into the living room.

He flops on the couch, sticks a cherry into his mouth, and talks with the fruit in his cheek while he picks up the TV remote. "Don't stop on my account," he mumbles. "Pretend I'm not here."

He flicks on the TV and starts flipping through the channels the way he did last night.

Taylor snaps out of his trance. "Hey—asshole! Whatever you think you're doing with Melody—you better understand she's mine! You keep your hands off her!"

Niko doesn't even look up. "I don't want her, man. You want her? Take her. I don't care."

"Hey!" Taylor snaps. "I'm talking to you! Turn off the damn TV!"

"The last time I checked, you were the one breaking and entering," Niko mutters between mouthfuls. "Why don't you take your woman in the other room? You'll be more comfortable there. You can shut the door and have all the privacy you want."

His attitude completely disarms Taylor. Taylor stares at him for a second, but Niko ignores him completely. Niko continues to munch his cherries and spit the seeds back into the box between changing the channels while he decides what to watch.

Taylor blinks at him a few more times and then turns back to me. He tries to lower his voice, but he has to speak over the noise from the TV.

"Come on, baby," Taylor insists. "Come with me right now. You don't have to stay here with him."

"I told you I can't, Taylor. I have to go through with this. My father needs this deal. You said you were okay with this....."

"Okay with it!" he snaps. "I was never okay with it! Are you telling me you would rather stay here with *him* than leave with me? What did you do—fuck him already? Are you taking this fake marriage thing seriously?"

I gasp in horror. "NO!! Of course not! I never did anything with Niko. He never tried anything....."

Taylor's expression goes hard. "I don't believe you. You wouldn't go to such lengths to stay in the same suite with him when I'm right here asking you to leave with me."

"I can't leave, Taylor! Don't you get that? There is nothing going on between me and Niko! Ask him. He'll tell you."

"I already told him," Niko calls over from the couch.

"You shut the hell up and stay out of this!" Taylor snaps over his shoulder. Then he turns back to me. "You're turning out to be as much of a tramp as I thought. I never should have believed you would stay faithful to me."

"Taylor!" I practically shriek.

Niko interrupts again. "Try treating a lady with a little more respect. You'll get further."

Taylor compresses his lips, but he doesn't turn around to confront Niko again.

Taylor glares at me. "We're finished. If you want to drag your bitch ass through the gutter with anyone who can pay your way, go right ahead. I'm done."

He storms past me toward the balcony. I yell at him one more time. "Taylor—no!"

He shakes me off too hard, walks out onto the balcony, and disappears. I don't know how he got here and I don't go over there to find out how he leaves.

I stare at the open balcony doors. Taylor is gone. He actually accused me of sleeping with Niko.

Niko and I got into that fight last night because I assumed he wanted to do it. Neither of us did and we didn't. We just watched a movie.

He was really nice about it. Now Taylor is coming around accusing me of the one thing I was the most concerned not to doing.

It's over between us. I don't want Taylor back if he could say things like that to me.

Was he only after my father's money after all? Did he say those things to break up with me—now that he knows he can't marry me himself?

I sink onto a divan near the balcony doors and stare at the floor. I can't believe this is happening. This is the perfect finale to an already disastrous situation.

I barely notice when Niko mutes the TV and comes over to sit next to me. "Don't listen to a word he says," Niko murmurs in my ear. "He's a jerk and you can do better."

I raise my hands, but I can't even fall apart the way I did last night. I'm too emotionally exhausted by all of this.

"Why did this have to happen?" I croak. "Everything would have been fine if my father hadn't pressured me into this fiasco of a marriage. Then I would be married to Taylor right now instead of you." I cover my eyes with my hand. "I'm sorry. I shouldn't have said that."

"Don't worry about it," he murmurs. "You don't have to apologize to me. I feel exactly the same way."

My shoulders slump. "I really appreciate all your kindness.....last night....and now..... I know this sucks for you as much as it does for me."

He snorts. "I'm sure it sucks much worse for you than it does for me. I'm sorry you got caught in all of this. It wasn't fair to you—and he didn't have to be such a jackass about it if he couldn't hack waiting for you." He stands up, goes back to the couch, and picks up the cherry box. "Do you want some? What do you want to do tonight?"

I sit there in a funk for a few more minutes, but I can't keep sulking forever—especially not when he's offering me a way out of it.

I go over to the couch, take a handful of cherries out of the box, and lean back on the couch to eat them.

"We watched my choice of movie last night," I tell him. "You pick tonight—or we could do something else. We don't have to watch a movie—or maybe you want to do something on your own. I don't expect you to do stuff with me."

He shrugs and spits out another cherry pit. "It is kinda relaxing to just sit around with no demands or expectations. I feel like I'm on vacation even though I'm still working."

I look up at him. "What about you? Do you have a girlfriend or someone special on the outside? I'm sorry I've been making this all about me when you could be in the same situation. I should have asked."

"No, I don't have a girlfriend." He puts the box in front of me and props his foot on the coffee table. He has to push some of the wedding gifts aside.

I look up at him. "You don't? I'm surprised."

"Why are you surprised? I'm not everyone's cup of tea."

"I mean.....you're rich, smart, good-looking, talented.....You said you can get any girl you want whenever you want. I'm surprised you don't have someone."

"That's what I meant. I can get any girl I want, but I don't want one. I have to fight them off with a stick."

I gape at the side of his face. "Why?! Why don't you want a girlfriend?"

"I was engaged and weeks away from getting married to the girl of my dreams when the deal fell through between me and your father. The whole disaster left me penniless and my fiancé dumped me and disappeared out of my life."

I'm too stunned even to speak. The horror of what he just said..... My father.....he robbed Niko of something so much more than money.

Does my father even realize what that deal cost Niko? No wonder Niko is so bitter about it. No wonder he hates everyone by the name of Gottlieb.

He glances over and sees me staring at him in stunned shock. He immediately looks away and pretends to change the TV channels even though the TV is muted.

"Anyway, it took me years to rebuild my fortune. I never let myself get involved with anyone else because I can't trust that they aren't after my money. Women throw themselves at me all the time, but I never let them get too close if I bother to deal with them at all. Most of the time I don't. I have more important things to think about. I can see right away that they're only attracted to my money. They wouldn't stick around if I was broke."

I force myself to look away. Those words sting.

I wouldn't be here if Niko was broke. My father, Dante, and everyone else never would have come up with this fake marriage idea if Niko was broke.

He and I are only together because of his money. No wonder he's so insistent that he wouldn't come near me—not for anything.

Chapter 12: Melody

Niko actually smiles when he offers me his arm. "Are you ready to knock 'em dead?"

I feel myself blushing. I smile back at him so much more easily now.

We're in this together. We work together as a team to get through every press spot. Now we have to get through another gala celebration at my father's mansion.

My eyes dip to Niko's tux. "You look like you're gonna knock 'em dead, too."

He smiles more broadly and his eyes make a similar darting movement down to my elaborate jeweled gown. "I'm sure I don't look as good as you do. Come on. Let's do this."

We walk out onto the balcony together. The press all over the ballroom floor snaps pictures of us. Niko and I wave at everyone.

Smiling for the cameras is so much easier, now that Niko and I aren't at each other's throats all the time. We made peace. We live together in our honeymoon suite. We spend the evenings together and talk.

He's really good company and he never judges anything. He treats me like a friend. He always puts me at ease and talks casually while we decide what we're going to do each evening.

I've never experienced this with anyone, not even with my father and Asher. Spending time with Niko feels like the easiest, most casual, most stress-free time of my life.

I actually dread the day when our pretend honeymoon comes to an end. Will he and I live apart after that?

I should ask him what he plans to do. I'm not engaged to Taylor anymore. I haven't even heard from him since he split up with me. I don't want to hear from him.

I have no reason not to keep living with Niko, but I suppose that's up to him.

I'm bracing myself for him to say he doesn't want to keep living with me. I can accept that. He never wanted this in the first place. Why should he continue with it?

He waits an appropriate amount of time for the reporters to finish taking all their pictures. Then he turns aside and leads me to the stairs.

We descend to the ballroom where everyone surrounds us shooting off questions about our plans, where we're going to live after the honeymoon, and all the details Niko and I haven't even discussed yet.

Getting through the wedding was hard enough. Now I don't know what the future holds.

How long does Niko plan to stay married to me before he divorces me? The thought makes me cringe.

I don't show it, though. I smile at everyone, get my picture taken a million times, and answer as many questions as I can. I have to keep the answers vague—mostly because I don't know the answers.

In a second, he leans in close to my ear. He has to yell to make himself heard. "Do you want something to eat or drink? I'm going to the buffet. I'll bring you something!"

I nod. He squeezes my hand and walks away.

Anyone watching him would think we were a real couple, but he's just being his usual gentlemanly self.

I get distracted by more reporters, more people congratulating me on my wedding, and even people asking me to introduce them to Niko so they can make business proposals to him.

I try to get out of these conversations as quickly and politely as possible. I don't know anything about Niko's business and I don't want to get involved in it.

I don't feel qualified to introduce anyone to him. I tell everyone to go introduce themselves. He's standing right over there.

I wave toward the buffet and spot him watching me from a distance. His eyes and facial expression don't blast hatred and murderous hostility anymore.

What is he thinking when he looks at me like that? Does he finally get it that I'm not part of whatever he hates so much about the Gottlieb family?

I can only hope. He's a good guy. I didn't see that before, but he has been nothing but kind and decent to me ever since that first night after the wedding.

He could have been a complete bastard to me. He could have said those things and left me crying in the corner by myself. He could have completely ignored me and not tried to help me at all.

The guests distract me again. I get pulled into the crowd. Niko doesn't come back, so maybe he got ambushed by his wanna-be business associates. Who knows?

I get preoccupied talking to Sabrina Rothschild. She introduces herself to me. I wouldn't have known who she was.

I start asking her about the Fabergé egg she gave us. She blows that off and starts describing all the eggs in her collection. She owns more than a hundred of them.

I'm astounded that I'm actually meeting someone this rich—but in the middle of the conversation, I hear another familiar voice behind me—actually two familiar voices.

I don't have to turn around to hear my father and Asher talking. I wouldn't have noticed that, either, except that they mention Holloway Industrial Carriers—Niko's trucking company.

"Global Trucking will cost more, but it will be worth it in the end if we can cut him out of the deal," Asher is saying.

"I can't afford to pay more," my father counters. "You were supposed to get inside his operation and find out when he schedules everything. This will be ten times harder without that information."

"No one can access that information unless they're a manager in the company—but it doesn't matter. All we have to do is schedule pickups and deliveries with Global. We can give Holloway Industrial different times—like say half an hour after Global picks up our goods. We can claim Holloway Industrial keeps showing up too late to fulfill its obligations and we have no choice but to use another trucking company. As soon as we drive him out, we can do our own fulfillment and start taking in his share of the profits."

"All right, son," my father replies. "You understand this better than I do. You make it happen for us."

Asher's tone changes. He tries to lower his voice to a confidential murmur, but he has to maintain a certain volume so my father can hear him over all the other noise in the ballroom.

"I'm already putting the wheels into motion," Asher tells him. "Niko will never know what hit him before he winds up on his ass with nothing."

I stiffen. So now Asher and my father are conniving to ruin Niko for the second time.

Niko says a lot of things about my father being too incompetent to run his own business.

That might be true, but now Asher is leading my father around by the nose. Asher probably wants to play on my father's desire for revenge so Asher can manipulate my father into taking over this deal.

I still don't turn around. I switch off my ears and try to concentrate on what Sabrina is saying.

She didn't make it easy because I have no interest in Fabergé eggs at all. What do I care about that?

My father and Asher were plotting against Niko. What can I do about this? Should I confront them—or tell Niko—or tell Dante?

Niko comes over to me just then. He hands me a champagne flute with one hand and a plate of nibbles with the other.

Sabrina introduced herself to him, and with no introduction at all, she launched into a business proposal idea she has for him to collaborate with her husband and brother-in-law.

Niko doesn't react. He listens in silence—or maybe I'm just too agitated to see him react. How can I keep this information from him, especially after the way he's been acting toward me these last few days?

He finally makes some non-committal statement like, "Send all the information through to my assistant and I'll take a look at it."

That delights Sabrina. She shakes his hand and leaves us alone—or as alone as we can possibly be in the middle of this gala.

Niko frowns at me. "Are you okay? You look like you're coming down with a stomach bug or something."

My hand flies to my head. "I need to sit down somewhere—somewhere quiet." I look around at everything without seeing anything.

"Come to the back room with me. We don't need to be here until the next press push."

He takes hold of my elbow and leads me across the ballroom. My father and Asher aren't there anymore—not in the same place where I overheard them talking.

My pulse starts pounding when Niko leads me away to the private room. He won't leave me alone in there. I'll be able to tell him what I heard.

Can I really do that? I went through with this fake marriage to help my father—and Asher is a part of that. Am I really about to rat them out to their worst enemy?

I didn't agree to screw Niko over. That wasn't part of the arrangement.

I might have been willing to consider it before the wedding. No way will I do it now.

Niko shuts the door behind us and pulls me down on the couch. "Sit down. Take a drink. You look like you're going to faint."

"Niko.....I have to tell you something."

He glances over at me. "Are you getting back together with Taylor? Did he come crawling back already?"

"Will you stop it?!" I practically shriek. "My father and Asher are planning to screw you over. They're planning to give you the wrong times for pickups and freight deliveries so your trucks arrive too late. Then Asher will arrange for Global Trucking to deliver the shipments and they'll be able to throw you out of the deal for breach of contract." I cover my face with both hands. "I can't believe I'm actually telling you this. My father is going to kill me."

He doesn't answer for what seems like a long time. The silence crushes my last nerve.

I can't keep sitting here with those words quivering in the air between us. I just betrayed my own family. I turned against my father and gave material aid to the enemy—or whatever term they use for it in the military.

I take my hands down, but I can't look at Niko. I pick up my champagne glass and pound the rest of my drink. I need another one, but I don't dare to leave the room.

Niko sits unnaturally still and quiet on the couch next to me. I feel him staring at me. Is he shocked? Is he horrified that I blurted all of that out to someone who is supposed to be an enemy of my family?

I dare to steal a peek at him. He doesn't even blink.

"Sorry," I mumble. "I should have just kept my mouth shut."

He shakes himself awake and leans back on the couch in his usual relaxed posture. "That makes a lot of sense. Thank you for telling me."

My head snaps up. "You knew about this?! And you let them get away with it?!"

"I didn't know the specifics. I knew Asher was up to something. I really appreciate you telling me. I won't forget this." He picks up my plate and hands it to me. "Are you hungry?"

I can't even look at the food. "What are you going to do about this? You can't let them cut you out like this."

"Don't worry about it. I'll handle it." He picks up one of the finger sandwiches from the plate and stuffs the whole thing into his mouth. "I owe you one for this. I mean it. I don't forget it when someone has my back like this."

"You'll handle it?!" I practically roar. "How will you handle it? How will you stop them from doing this?"

"It's simple. I'll just track your father's shipments myself. I'll be able to tell when he's bringing in shipments of goods. I'll be able to adjust our timetable so our trucks get there first to take on the cargo. It's a piece of cake."

"Well.....what are you going to do about Asher.....and my father?! They're both involved in this—and you're stuck in business with people who want to stab you in the back."

He makes a face, bites into a celery stick, and licks the rest of the dip off the plate. "I don't think your father was behind this. I think Asher is the one pulling puppet strings on your father. Asher came to my office the other day trying to get logistical information on my truck movements. I knew he was up to no good. Now I know why. Don't worry. You have nothing to be concerned about. I'm one step ahead of them—thanks to you." He studies me a little more closely. "Are you ready to go back to the gala?"

I stare at him in dazed confusion. He gazes straight back into my eyes. He really isn't concerned about this at all.

How does a man become so confident and self-possessed in the face of such a blatant attack? I have never seen anyone act like this.

I become aware in that moment that he and I are sitting too close on the couch—close enough to kiss.

He could kiss me or put his arm around me if we were a real couple, but we aren't.

My eyes dart down to his mouth. He's really good-looking—and he has a personality to match. All those women who chase him for his money—they don't know what they're missing.

Am I the only woman alive who knows what a sweet, caring, protective gentleman he is behind closed doors? He never shows this side to anyone—not anyone female, at least.

His eyes match mine and he looks down at my mouth, but he turns away without doing anything.

He picks up my empty plate and glass, holds out his hand, and says, "Let's get back out there. Just stay close to me. No one will bother you as long as we're together."

I take his hand. I've been holding his hand in public a lot lately. I've been holding his hand or his arm almost the entire time we've been together here tonight.

Holding his hand or walking around on his arm makes me feel like we really are a couple. I feel like I could actually care that much about him.

He doesn't want that and neither do I. This whole fake marriage is complicated enough as it is.

We head back out to the gala, take our places on the ballroom floor, and field a bunch of other questions, congratulations, and business proposals from a bunch of people I've never laid eyes on before.

Asher and my father keep their distance from Niko, which means they keep their distance from me, too.

I hold onto his hand and stay close to him. I don't want to deal with them. I couldn't face them.

At least he's here and he knows now. His presence makes me feel better. Nothing bad can happen to me as long as I stay near him.

So how is that going to work when we stop living together?

Chapter 13: Melody

I topple onto the couch in the honeymoon suite living room. "Oh, my God!" I groan. "My feet are killing me!"

I kick off my heels, fold my legs under me on the couch, and rub my aching feet. I've been standing in those heels for hours at the gala. My bones throb and my ankle tendons feel twisted.

Niko goes over to the fridge, pulls the ice cream out of the freezer, and comes over with two spoons. He scoops out a bite, puts it into his mouth, and hands me the carton.

"Don't you ever stop eating?" I tease.

He laughs. "I stop eating all the time when I'm working. I don't eat at work, so I have to make up for it outside of work."

"Why don't you eat at work?" I rotate the carton around. "Pecan praline! That's my favorite."

"The ice cream gods were smiling on you. I don't eat because I'm too focused on what I'm doing. I don't feel hungry and I don't want to stop what I'm doing."

"It sounds like a cross between a really good weight-loss strategy and an eating disorder."

He laughs again and takes another bite. "Don't worry. I'll be packing on enough calories during this honeymoon to last me until next spring." His eyes twinkle when he hands back the carton. "I can't say the same thing for you."

"You bastard!" I pretend to kick him, but I really only nudge him in the leg with my bare foot. I don't even have the energy to change out of my dress and get into my pajamas.

He takes one more bite and leans back. "That's enough for me. You can finish the rest." He picks up the streaming guide. "What do you want to do tonight—watch another movie?"

"I think we've watched everything on there that either of us is interested in."

"Far from it. We've just watched everything on here that both of us are interested in. There is plenty on here that I'm interested in that I'm certain you aren't."

"Really? Like what? Try me."

"*Kill Bill Parts 1 & 2* are on here. *The Professional* is on here. *Escape From New York* is on here. I could watch any or all of them."

"Sure. We could watch them," I reply. "I like all of those."

He almost drops the guide. "You do?"

"Of course." I laugh at him. "I like all kinds of movies as long as they're good. I've seen all of those before. I could definitely watch them again."

He raises his eyebrows and puts the guide down. "You're full of surprises, aren't you?"

"I'm not trying to be full of surprises. If we're stuck here, we might as well do something we both enjoy."

He nods at the carton in my hand. "Are you done? I could put it away if you've had enough."

I hand it to him and he puts it back in the freezer before he returns to his place.

"I don't feel like watching another movie," he decides.

"What do you want to do instead? I suppose we could always play 20 Questions."

He rolls his eyes. "What are you—seven?"

Now it's my turn to laugh. "Seriously. What are you going to do about Asher?"

He only shrugs like my question doesn't surprise him at all. "I'll just have to keep an eye on him until he removes himself from my orbit."

"How does that work? He won't remove himself. He'll just keep causing you problems—and don't even get me started on Daddy."

"Guys like that always remove themselves. They always make one mistake too many and take themselves down. I don't have to do anything. Their own incompetence causes their undoing."

I shake my head and look away. "I hate it that you're talking about my father like that, but I can't come up with any argument against it."

He looks over at me. "You don't have to take my word for it. It's all right there in the public record. You could look into the details of his deal with me. You'll find out for yourself that I'm telling the truth."

I wince. I can't look at him. "I don't have to—especially not after tonight. I already had a gut feeling that you were telling the truth, but tonight confirmed it."

He remains silent for a minute while he studies me from the other end of the couch. I should gracefully bow out of this conversation with my dignity intact—if I have any dignity left at all.

Without warning, he extends his hand down the couch cushions, takes hold of my bare foot, and starts massaging it with deep, penetrating squeezes.

I freeze when I feel him touching me—and then the flood of ecstasy overwhelms me. I collapse back on the cushions groaning in relief. "Oh, my God!"

He chuckles to himself and pulls my foot into his lap. His powerful fingers and hand muscles twist, knead, and rub all the tension and aching pain out of my feet.

I topple backward and my eyes slip out of focus. I've never felt anything like this in my life.

He rubs up to my ankle and up to my calf before he takes hold of my other foot. He pulls it down into his lap, too, to I have to stretch out on the couch.

I open my eyes to find him drilling me from a few feet away. The intensity of his stare bores straight into my being.

His eyes smolder with hidden fire. His power makes me tremble. I can't deny anymore that he isn't just giving me an innocent foot massage.

The instant I make that connection, his touch changes. He crawls his hands higher up my legs, squeezes my thighs above my knees, and pushes my dress up.

I see myself sprawled in front of him in this flimsy dress. He can see every detail of my body underneath.

My breath catches when I realize a second too late what he's about to do. A rush of heat shoots between my legs and my whole body softens in his hands.

He eases his hot, strong hands under my dress, takes hold of my panties, and slides them down. My dress covers me. He can't see anything—not of my body, at least.

He sees me vibrating with buried desire. Just being around him excites me. Now he's looking at me like that while his hands travel all over me.

He stays on the outside of my dress and strokes up my legs to my hips, surrounds my waist just for a moment, and then grips my ribs just below my breasts.

His masterful hands command me to respond. His eyes never release me. We both know what we're doing and what this means.

He caresses his flat palm down my stomach to my quivering mound under my dress. I'm not wearing any panties. Does he realize how hot and wet he makes me when he touches me like that?

He leaves his hand there just for a second and then drops his thumb between my swollen lips to rub my clitoris.

I pant in an agony of desire. My body writhes in front of him. I can't stop myself from showing him how much I need this.

I need to release all the tension that has been building up since this whole thing started. All the hostility between me and Niko comes to a boiling point right now.

We went through the wedding disaster. Then Taylor dumped me and Niko and I have been getting closer ever since. He's the nicest guy I've ever met—and by far the hottest.

He watches me from high above. He sees my lips shivering with every ragged breath. He sees me spasm when he hits my clitoris in just the right way. He knows he turns me on and that I want him to take me.

He scoops his other hand up to my breasts and makes me moan when he grips it hard through my dress. I heave in his grasp. I don't even care that he knows how much I want him.

He doesn't stop fingering me when he rakes his fingertips up to my shoulder and pulls the strap of my dress down. He scoots it all the way off my breasts and exposes them for him to play with.

I whine and flinch when he pinches and twists them. I want him to handle me as his own. I want him to take what he wants and leave me sobbing for more. I need this so damn bad! I've never needed a man as much as this.

He fights his features under control while he watches me. He keeps clenching his jaw and compressing his lips to hold back whatever reaction he's having to my naked desire.

I spiral my hips into his hand to make him release me, but he never picks up his pace or rubs harder. He stays soft, gentle, and maddeningly slow. Will he ever take what he wants? Does he even want me at all?

He stops rubbing me and I cry out in desperation when he slips his hand up my dress. His fingers slither into my wetness and plunge home to split me apart.

I scream and then moan in ecstasy as he drills his fingers in deeper than deep. He satisfies something so magnificently hungry in me. I need all of him right now.

I thrash on the couch trying to spread my legs to take him deeper, but this position won't let me. I'm a captive of my own desire.

I spiral off into an epic climax. I have to turn my face aside and shut my eyes from the intensity of everything I'm feeling right now.

I'm still reeling in the stratosphere and praying he finishes me off when he lunges forward. He keeps his hand buried all the way inside me when he lies down on top of me and drives his pelvis down behind his hand.

He attacks my mouth kissing me fast and hard. His tongue invades my mind and his hot breath sears my brain with so much fire that I can't stand it.

His iron body arches into his thrusts, but he doesn't take his clothes off. He plants his other hand above my head and uses it as leverage to pump his fingers in again and again.

He gasps between breaths. Every tortured inhalation rasps with buried passion and excruciating desire.

I want him more than ever, now that he's prepared me for him.

I break off his mouth and stare up into those molten eyes glaring down at me from above. I have to touch him. I have to feel him.

I grab his belt and pull it loose. He doesn't stop pumping when I dive my hand down his shorts and my fingers close on his thick, hard, rock-solid meat.

His nostrils flare when I squeeze and then I start stroking. He thrusts harder into my hand. I feel that slab of hot iron driving into me when he arches his hips against his own knuckles. This isn't his fingers inside me. It's him.

His eyes glaze as he picks up speed and power. His skin rolls between my fingers. His shaft spasms with each deep thrust.

He feels incredible in my hand. I want to take him—but some part of me already knows we won't go there.

He groans once, dives in to kiss me, and then bellows in my mouth as he releases into my hand.

His whole body convulses in tormented spasms. His hot load drenches my hand before he collapses on top of me.

He falls with his face buried in the cushion behind my head. He sinks into my hair and lies there panting and shaking for a minute.

I want to put my arms around him and make it all okay, but he tears himself off far too soon.

He draws his fingers out of me and his movements pull my hand out of his pants.

He sits back down in the same place, runs his fingers through his hair, and rests his head in his hand while he stares down at the floor.

I stare at him from the same place on the couch. My juices cool on my thighs and ass. Does he regret what we just did? I don't.

I sit up, but I don't say anything to him. What can I say—thank you? That's what I want to say, but I don't want to disturb him.

I can't read his reaction. I don't want to impose myself on him, especially if this was just a moment of physical release for him. I'll be happy to just forget it if it was.

This doesn't change anything between us. I'm not what he wants and he isn't what I want. We're just ships passing in the night.

It felt good in the moment for both of us. That's all it was—a moment.

My panties lie on the floor next to the couch. I slither my dress down and pull the straps up to my shoulders to cover myself.

I should go change, but I don't want to walk out without saying something to him.

I make up my mind, grab the room service menu from the table behind the couch, and pull out my phone.

"Do you want to order Chinese food tonight?" I ask. "They also have pizza, Italian, and fried chicken. My vote is Chinese. What do you think?"

He runs his fingers through his hair again before he looks up. He looks dazed. At least he doesn't look angry, hurt, or resentful.

"Yeah, Chinese would be good." He sits back on the couch and puts his arm over the back to face me from a polite social distance. "Good idea."

I smile at him and call room service to place the order.

"I'm gonna go change," I tell him. "I'll be back in a minute."

He says, "Okay," and I go to my room.

I come out wearing my pajamas. Niko has changed, too. He wears a pair of navy blue sweatpants, a thick pair of wool socks, and a black hoodie. He looks so much more accessible like this—like he's just a normal guy instead of a hyper-rich business tycoon.

I'm just coming out of my room when he meets the room service waiter at the door. Niko tips the guy and wheels the cart into the living room.

We put everything on the coffee table in front of the couches, sit down with our plates and forks, and he picks up the TV remote. "So what will it be?" he asks. *"Kill Bill, Escape from New York,* or *The Professional?"*

"Let's go with *Kill Bill*—and I promise I won't recite the dialogue this time."

"Go right ahead. It doesn't bother me."

I look over at him and he smiles. He starts the movie and we spend the opening sequence serving ourselves our food.

He holds out his arm to me when we sit back on the cushions. "Come here," he tells me.

I scoot closer and he pulls me against his shoulder. He puts his arm around me and cuddles me against his side while the movie starts.

We both eat our food and occasionally lean forward to get more. Then we both sit back together. This is so nice. I'm really starting to love spending time with him.

Chapter 14: Niko

I check my trucking company app to make sure all our orders and deliveries are on schedule. Then I go back to reading spreadsheets on all my companies, their operations, expenses, and revenue streams.

Ray sits on the couch across the office doing something on his phone. We're both too busy to talk. We haven't said a word to each other in over two hours.

I'm just changing spreadsheets when I get another call from Emory. "Now what?" I ask. "I'm a little busy."

"You might want to stop what you're doing," he murmurs under his breath. "You have another unannounced visitor."

"Oh, please, Dear God tell me it isn't Asher Gottlieb again."

"No, it's Gottlieb Senior," Emory whispers. "And Dante Helme is with him. They insist on seeing you immediately. Dante says it's critical."

I stop what I'm doing, all right. If Dante says it's critical, it must be. "Holy crap!" I gasp. "Send them in."

I stand up and button my jacket so I'm ready when they come in. I even walk out from behind my desk and meet them at the door.

I shake hands with Dante. Then I shake hands with Saul.

"Thank you for seeing us at such short notice," Dante tells me. "Believe me, we wouldn't have come if it wasn't important."

"Don't mention it. My door is always open to you two. Take a seat." I step back behind my desk, but I don't sit down. "What can I do for you?"

Neither of them sits down, either. They remain standing and square their shoulders at me across my desk. "We just discovered evidence that your brother Ray is building an alternate marketplace from mine," Dante tells me.

"And he's courting my suppliers behind my back," Saul cuts in. "He's trying to cut us both out of business and corner the whole deal for you! He's already placed orders for the same goods from the same supplier. He's using his own name to hide it from you."

I allow myself to relax. "Oh, that. Yeah, I know about that."

"You know?!" Saul practically bellows. "Did you put him up to this?!" He rounds on Dante. "I told you something like this was going to happen....."

"I didn't put him up to it," I tell him. "I found out a few days ago."

Ray shoots off the couch. "How can you go along with this?! You don't actually believe this, do you? I'm your brother! We've done business together for years! They're lying! They're making it all up to drive us apart!"

"It's all true!" Saul spits over his shoulder and turns on me. "I swear to Christ, if I find out you're behind this or even participating in it...."

"I already handled it, Saul. You have nothing to worry about. It isn't a problem."

"What do you mean—you handled it?" Saul and Dante ask at the same time.

"You can't believe this bullshit, man!" Ray insists. "They're both liars."

Dante narrows his eyes at the guy. "Call me a liar one more time and you'll never see the light of day again."

I hold out my hand to him. "Keep your shorts on, man. I told you. It's all taken care of."

"You still haven't explained what that means," Dante counters. "We have proof that we're telling the truth."

"You don't need it because I have all the proof already. I found the purchase orders in his name, the invoices for the web marketplace, and the brick-and-mortar retail outlets he plans to use to circumvent both of you."

"Then how can you stand there and act so blasé about all of this?!" Saul demands. "We won't have a business if this goes through! You'll be the last man standing—which is obviously what he wants."

"I told you not to worry about it. I'm not blasé about it. I just know it doesn't mean anything because none of that is going to go through."

"What are you talking about?" Ray gasps. "What did you do?"

"You don't have access to the bank accounts you planned to use to pay for all of those orders. You know I've been moving my assets into a trust to protect them from this whole marriage thing. Well, the bank accounts are in the trust now, too—and your name isn't on any of them. You won't be able to pay for the purchase of the goods. You won't be able to pay for the web marketplaces. You won't be able to rent premises for brick-and-mortar retail outlets. You got nothing, brother. You're out on your ass—which is better than you deserve considering that you tried to screw me over."

Ray gapes at me with his jaw on the floor. "What?! You can't do this to me!"

"Oh, and that company car you drive and the penthouse downstairs from mine—I rekeyed them both. You don't have access to them or the contents of the penthouse, including your clothes. Your actions cost the company thirty thousand dollars—so I'm repossessing the contents of the penthouse to balance your debt."

He blinks at me and then gulps. Dante turns around and laughs in his face. "Suck on it, you piece of shit."

"Niko....." Ray chokes. "I'm your brother......"

"You should have thought of that before you shit in my bed. I'm giving you one hour to leave the building and take nothing with you but your phone and the clothes on your back. Service to your phone will cut off at the end of the month. That's two weeks from now. I suggest you use that time to get yourself another job—if you can. You won't get a reference from anyone in any of my companies. Don't come around me. Don't show your face to me. You'll never screw me over or anyone else again as long as I can do anything about it." I pretend to check my watch. "Your hour starts now."

Ray stands there staring at me in horror. I don't even feel bad for him when Dante and Saul both laugh at his shocked reaction.

Ray finally backs away, trips over his own feet, and stumbles out of the office.

Dante comes toward me grinning and sticks out his hand. "That was absolutely savage. I'm impressed. Thank you. I should have known you wouldn't let us down."

"Of course not. Allow me to apologize for his rude remarks."

"You don't have to apologize for anything."

Saul steps forward and shakes my hand laughing in nervous relief. "I've never seen anything like that before."

"I'm sorry it came to this." I give him a pointed look. "Let's make sure nothing like this happens again on either side."

"Of course, of course," he says way too fast and shakes my hand again.

Dante won't stop laughing and shaking his head. "That one is going down in the history books."

"Let's hope it doesn't. Is there anything else I can do for either of you?"

"That covers it." Dante shakes my hand again. "Thank you."

They both leave and I sit back down in my chair. I try to concentrate on my work, but the eerie silence won't let me.

Ray isn't here anymore. He was a thorn in my side for years. I knew a long time ago that I couldn't trust him—not the way I should have been able to trust someone that close to me.

I should have gotten rid of him ages ago, but I just couldn't bring myself to swing the hammer down.

I could have called up countless other incidents where he stabbed me in the back—or tried to. Today was just the latest of many—and maybe the worst.

Anyway, it's over. He won't come back to the office. He won't come back to the penthouse. He's out.

He might be smart enough to leave town and start over where no one knows him.

Then again, he might just be arrogant and self-obsessed enough to actually try to rebuild here in New York.

He won't be able to. He'll only ruin himself if he tries.

This town is too small, especially in the business world. Saul and Dante will spread the word about Ray. No one will ever trust him again.

Word will get out that his own brother threw him out with nothing. That on its own says all any respectable businessman needs to know.

My reputation is still spotless. If it comes down to people choosing to put their faith in me or Ray, they'll choose me. No question.

I turn my desk chair around and stare out the window. I don't like that I had to throw him out. I don't like that I had to humiliate him in front of two other businessmen.

I'm glad I did it in front of Dante. He deserved to see Ray brought down in the harshest way possible.

Saul deserved that, too, but Dante means more to me. I'll always have to do right by him.

I know for certain now that Saul is in on Asher's plot to screw me over. Saul won't repay my deeds today with the same consideration. Saul won't lift a finger to rein in Asher.

That's someone else's problem now. I'm already doing everything necessary to protect myself.

I won't be the person going down in flames when the shit hits the fan. I don't know who will be. It will probably be Saul.

I can't pity the guy. He made his bed. Now he's gonna lie in it. He's just too short-sighted to see it coming before it hits him with a sledgehammer.

Chapter 15: Melody

I sit cross-legged on the couch in the honeymoon suite—or is it the bridal suit? I don't even know anymore.

I go through the wedding gifts arranged on the coffee table and write out my thank-you cards while the TV plays *The Blues Brothers* in the background.

I get butterflies in my stomach when I think about Niko coming home from work. This isn't home, but I still get excited about seeing him again.

Last night's make-out session keeps playing in my mind. It was one of the hottest experiences of my life and we didn't even do it.

He is definitely hot. He turns me on more than Taylor—more than any guy I've ever known.

The close moments on the couch afterward mean more, though. That was such a special experience—just sitting close to him with his arm around me, sharing our Chinese food, and watching a movie together.

Could this thing between us be real? Could it ever become real? Does he even want that?

He was engaged. He was going to marry the woman of his dreams.

Some part of him must want that. He only gave it up because he couldn't trust anyone not to go after him for his money.

I'm starting to understand his point of view. He has more money than God. He definitely has more money than my father.

Niko is at the top of the pyramid. He said women throw themselves at him all the time, but they only want his money.

That must make it extremely hard to trust anyone. Maybe he thinks no one will or even can understand him without getting blinded by his money.

He might be right about that. Some people won't see anything else. Most people won't see anything else.

I put my card in the envelope, lick it to seal it, and scribble the address on the front cover. I lay the envelope aside and pick up my next card when my phone rings.

The call is from Asher. "We're sending a limo around to pick you up, sweetheart. We need you to come over and meet us. We have to talk to you."

"Us?" I asked. "Do you mean you and Daddy?"

"Of course. Go down to the lobby. The limo will be there soon."

I hang up, put my thank-you cards away, put my phone in my purse, and ride the elevator down to the lobby.

I'm already dressed in one of my nicer outfits. I don't want to slum it in front of Niko anymore—not unless we're cuddling up in our pajamas. I want to look nice when he comes home.

I sure hope this meeting with Asher and my father doesn't last long. I don't want Niko to come home and find me not there.

I shouldn't be thinking of us as a real couple—not just because we made out one time.

He was the one who pulled me in to cuddle on the couch afterward. I didn't do that. I would have been ready to leave it alone for the rest of eternity.

I get to the lobby just as the limo pulls up in front of the hotel. The chauffeur opens the door for me and I get in. I'm all alone in this enormous car.

I pull out my phone on the way back to my father's house. I check the time. I still have three more hours before Niko is supposed to come home.

I don't want to tell him where I'm going. I don't want him to think I'm conniving with my father and Asher behind his back.

If they are conniving, I'll just tell Niko the way I did last time. I won't let them use this marriage against him—or against me.

The limo purrs into the driveway and the chauffeur lets me out in front of the grand entrance. I go upstairs to my father's office where I find him and Asher waiting for me.

My father comes toward me beaming and holds out both his arms to hug me. "Darling!" he exclaims and kisses me on the cheek. "You're free! Your nightmare is over!"

"Um....what are you talking about?" I have to turn aside to hug Asher. "Why are you two acting all affectionate all of a sudden?"

"We can dissolve this stupid marriage now!" my father exclaims. "You don't have to go back."

I furrow my brow. "What in the world are you talking about?"

"We did it! Don't you see?" my father gushes.

"No, Daddy. I don't see. How could I see when you haven't explained it to me?"

"We cut Niko out of the deal," Asher tells me. "We switched to Global Trucking so we don't have to use Holloway Industrial to ship our goods to Dante's retail distribution network." He spreads his hands and grins at me. "See? Niko is penniless. Global Trucking costs us more, but it's worth it to get rid of him. Now we don't owe him anything."

My father squeezes both my hands. "We can dissolve the marriage now. You can marry Taylor the way you planned and everything will be perfect."

I'm too stunned to react when he kisses me on the cheek again. "You....Don't you have a contract with Niko—and Dante?" I ask. "Doesn't the contract require you to use Holloway Industrial?"

"It requires Holloway Industrial to give us a competitive rate. Niko didn't do that, so technically, he was the one who breached our contract first. That released us from upholding our obligation. We're free to seek other shipping channels elsewhere."

"But you just said Global costs you more. So Niko *was* giving a competitive rate. He never breached the contract in the first place. You did!"

My father pulls my hands to steer me in a different direction. He won't stop beaming at me in blushing rapture. "You don't need to concern yourself with that, my dear. The important thing is that Niko is out of the deal."

Asher gives a sick laugh. "We ruined him for good this time. He'll never bounce back from this."

I look back and forth between these two men—my father and my brother. They're my flesh and blood—the only family I have.

Niko was telling the truth. My father did screw him over the first time. My father has been lying about that and playing the victim card ever since.

Did he and Asher concoct this whole deal to destroy Niko a second time? Is that what my marriage to Niko is—an elaborate plot—for what?

I can't even call it revenge because Niko was the injured party the first time. He would be the one looking for revenge, but he isn't.

He has treated me like a queen since the wedding and even before. He never threatened me—not the way I threatened him.

He told me the truth about my father. I was too blind and deaf to see and hear it then.

The grins on my father's and brother's faces make me sick. They really did this. They ruined Niko—for nothing.

My father sold me out just to conclude a shady business deal. I mean nothing to him—not compared to whatever criminal schemes he's running behind the thin green curtain.

Asher is right there in my father's pocket. Asher doesn't care about me, either. I'm a commodity to both of them—a commodity they don't mind auctioning off whenever it suits them.

I'm not even a valuable commodity. I'm not even a dollar amount. I'm less than that.

My father pulls me down into a chair, but I'm too numb to listen to what he's saying.

"We'll draw up all the paperwork for the dissolution. You and Niko haven't been married long enough to need a full divorce. We can just annul the marriage. It will be as if it never happened." My father kisses me on the forehead. "You can go back to the honeymoon suite, pack your suitcases, and then call the limo to bring you home. You're free, my darling. Our plan worked. I'm so proud of you."

I stumble out of the house, get back into the limo, and ride back to the Mandarin Oriental in a trance. Niko is broke—again. He probably doesn't even know it yet.

How long will it take before he figures it out? How long does he have before the axe falls and all the creditors come knocking on his door?

He has to stand aside and watch his whole empire crumble before his eyes. He has to watch all his blood, sweat, and tears slip through his fingers—and for what?

My family did that to him—twice.

He'll rebuild it. He's too strong, smart, and resourceful to let something like this keep him down.

He'll rebuild the way he did the first time. He came back ten times stronger, got a hundred times richer, and now everyone in the New York business world respects him for it.

Does Dante know about Niko's history with my father? Does Dante know my father was the one who ruined that first deal?

I can't imagine Dante putting Niko and my father together in another business arrangement if Dante really knew the truth.

He probably just heard the mutual accusations and excused himself from judgment on either side. That makes more sense.

I replay Niko's story in my mind. His fiancé dumped him when he lost everything. She left him in pieces because he didn't have any money.

That isn't going to be me. I can be there for him the way she wasn't. I can support him through this. I'll show him that I'm serious and that I don't just value him for his wealth.

Chapter 16: Niko

I pass my key card in front of the lock to open the door to the honeymoon suit. I get a face full of the delicious smell of pasta sauce, roasting vegetables, and homemade garlic bread.

I stop in the doorway and stare at Melody buzzing around the kitchen. She wears a white chef's apron over a cute, short skirt and a button-down blouse tied tight around her narrow waist.

She looks up and bursts into a huge, beaming smile when she sees me. "Hi!" she gasps.

"Hi......" I stammer. "What are you doing?"

"I'm making dinner. I hope you're hungry—and I really hope you like Italian."

"I am Italian. Why are you making dinner? We could have just ordered room service instead."

"I wanted to make it. I scavenged the pantry and fridge, collected all the food we have in the suite, and combined it into this!" She waves at the pots and pans billowing steam from the stove.

Just then, the timer goes off on the oven. She spins around, grabs a hot mitt, and pulls the garlic bread out of the oven.

I dare to take a step closer. "Where did you learn to cook like this?"

She laughs. I've never seen her like this. She absolutely glows with happiness. "I used to sneak into the kitchen and watch the chef and his team making the meals at home. Then, one day, he noticed me and asked if I wanted to help out. We had to keep it a secret from my father, but I really loved going down there and working in the kitchen. It was f un!"

I stand back and I have to admit that she really does know what she's doing. She drains pasta into the sink, combines it with sauce, and puts it all back into the oven to bake it into a casserole.

Then she whizzes around the room setting the table for two. She even lights two candles in the middle—I guess to try to make it romantic.

"Is this some kind of trick?" I ask.

She laughs again. "Only if you aren't hungry. Sit down. Do you want me to make you something to drink?"

I can't just sit here and let her serve me a drink—not on top of everything she's already doing.

I cross the living room to the wine fridge under the kitchen counter next to the regular fridge. I hunt around. "Does any of this contain meat?"

"The pasta sauce has beef, sausage, and ground lamb—and the salad has shrimp in it."

"That sounds like we need a red." I pull one of the bottles out of the wine fridge. I inspect the label and take down two glasses.

I pour for both of us and hand hers across the counter. I don't know if I should be getting too close when she's acting so differently.

I sip my wine while I watch her. She smirks at me over the rim of her glass when she takes a sip. Then she has to get back to work.

"Did something happen today?" I ask. "Something that made you want to cook dinner for us?"

She smiles even more broadly. She's definitely blushing. "Let's just say I really liked chilling on the couch with you last night. It was really sweet—and I wanted to show my appreciation for how kind you've been to me since we got married. So I decided to do this."

I don't answer. I didn't do anything out of the ordinary last night—apart from making out with her and both of us getting off together.

That was nothing. It was certainly not enough to warrant this response.

She keeps dashing back and forth between the kitchen and the table. She stops every now and then to sip her wine.

"I hope you aren't a lightweight," I tell her.

She blushes again. "I wish I could say I am, but all that champagne I've been drinking lately definitely boosted my tolerance. Don't worry. You won't wind up sitting next to me while I puke in the bathroom."

Now it's my turn to laugh. "Thank God for that."

She waves her hot mitt at me. "Come sit down. We can eat now."

She puts all the food into nice dishes she scrounged from the kitchen. She serves everything onto the table along with serving utensils, takes off her apron, and finally brings over the wine bottle.

She's beaming in happiness when she sits down opposite me. She raises her glass and touches it to mine. "Here's to you, Niko. Thank you for being such a prince these last few days. I'm actually glad I got roped into this deal so I could meet you. It has been......truly eye-opening."

She sips her wine, puts down her glass, and starts serving me. I don't know what to think. I don't see myself as a prince just because I treated her like a decent human being.

I put my glass down. She actually stands up so she can serve me. She loads my plate completely before she sits down and serves herself.

Her eyes keep sparkling at me from across the table. What am I supposed to make of all of this?

I feel like I'm on a date with someone I didn't even ask out. No one has ever gone so over the top for me before. Does this mean anything? Should I read anything into this?

I can't see anything about what she's doing that isn't the same as something she would do just to express her appreciation for someone who helped her through a difficult time.

I could easily see this as a platonic gesture with no hidden subtext at all—but there is a hidden subtext. I just don't know what it is—or maybe I'm the one who is reading hidden subtext into it.

She's beautiful, charming, and she obviously thinks the world of me. She had my back when she told me about her father and Asher plotting against me.

That means a lot. It means a hell of a lot more than this dinner.

Telling me must have cost her a lot. She had to turn against her own family to do the right thing by me—and she did it easily. She did it without any prompting. She volunteered the information on her own initiative.

I want to trust her. I want to believe she could actually do something like that for me again—maybe all the time.

I can't trust her completely. I barely know her—but she sure is tempting. Her personality is the most tempting thing about her.

Even the way she hated me at the beginning makes me trust her. She hated me because I came between her and Taylor. She was rock-solid loyal to him even after the wedding.

She never looked sideways at me. She was prepared to defend herself so she could stay loyal to him. She stayed loyal to him right up until the moment he dumped her for no reason.

He's an idiot if he didn't see how much she cared about him. A loyal woman is too rare. You don't just throw one away when she dedicates herself to you.

Melody would be like that for any man she got together with. She would commit herself and stay the course. She stayed engaged to him for a year before this whole deal threw a wrench in the works.

She sees me watching her. "How was your day?" she asks. "Did anything happen for you at work?"

I shrug that away. "Nothing worth mentioning. I had a meeting with Dante and your father about the deal. That's all."

She freezes to her chair. "You had a meeting with them—and it was nothing worth mentioning?"

Her sudden change in attitude sets my alarm bells ringing, but I make an effort not to show it. "No, it wasn't. Why? Should it have been?"

"So....the deal.....is everything going the way you planned?"

"Everything is going the way the contract says it should go. Everything seems to be working so far. Time will tell, though." I study her again. Why does she ask about that?

She shakes it off and stabs her fork into a piece of sausage buried in pasta sauce. Everything she made is delicious. I should probably tell her that.

"This is one of the best meals I've ever eaten," I tell her. "Thank you. It's way better than room service."

She turns bright red. "I'm glad you like it. We're only staying here for a little while longer. I'm going to have to get creative with the ingredients we have left."

Now it's my turn to freeze to the chair. "You....you plan to cook for us from now on?"

"If you want me to....if you like the food. It's cheaper this way—cheaper than getting room service every night."

I can't stop myself from frowning. Why is she suddenly worried about how cheap it is?

She distracts me by picking up the wine bottle. "Do you want some more?"

I nod. She pours me a glass before we both go back to eating.

I'm missing some crucial piece of the puzzle here—something that explains the way she's acting.

The weirdest part is that she seems so happy. She seems a thousand times happier about cooking for me than she was about any other part of this whole crazy situation.

So she's doing this to save money. Why? And why would saving money this way make her so happy? It doesn't compute.

We talk casually through the rest of the meal. She tells me to relax while she cleans the kitchen.

She bustles around loading the dishwasher and scrubbing out all the pots and pans. She actually smiles to herself while she does it—like that really makes her happy, too.

I don't believe what I'm seeing, but I have to.

Chapter 17: Niko

Melody dries her hands, takes off her apron, switches off the kitchen lights, and brings her wine glass over to the couch.

She sits down in the usual place—at a respectable, platonic distance from me. She doesn't throw herself at me—not that she ever did. I was the one who initiated last time.

She tucks her feet under her skirt, swivels sideways, and smiles down the couch at me. "So what's tonight's excitement?"

"What floats your boat?" I ask. "We would probably start growing moss if we watch movies every night."

She bursts out laughing and her cheeks color. "We wouldn't want that, would we? I could give *you* a foot massage. You gave me one last night. I could reciprocate."

The hair stands up on the back of my neck. Was that a come-on? Is she trying to start something with me?

Would it be so bad if she did? My mind switches to last night. I wouldn't mind doing that with her again. She's hot as hell when she gets going.

I pretend to shrug. "Okay. That would be great."

I kick off one of my shoes, pull my sock off, and stick my bare foot down the couch in her direction.

She puts her wine glass on the coffee table, adjusts her position, and starts rubbing my foot.

She has small, delicate hands. They're still warm from the dishwater. She's a lot stronger than I expected.

Her hands melt me into a puddle of goo. I collapse back on the cushions with a groan of pure pleasure. "Oh, my God! You are so hired."

She laughs again. "Is it too hard?"

"No, it's perfect. Oh, my God! Don't ever stop."

She keeps giggling at my reaction. She rubs hard, drives her knuckle down the sole of my foot, and twists my toes to work all the tension out of my feet.

I didn't realize my feet were so tense. Her fingers send jets of sensation up my legs—and I start getting turned on.

I try to play it off by taking off my other shoe and sock. I put both my legs on the couch. She beams at me when she starts rubbing my other foot.

I can't stop growling and groaning as she kneads my feet to soft, rubbery comfort. I've never felt anything like this.

She doesn't stop. She keeps going, rubs my ankles and my heels, and works her powerful fingers into the muscles connecting my feet to my legs.

I can't deal with this. I realize in that moment. I don't want tonight to be a platonic expression of appreciation. I want more.

I drag my eyes open and see her smiling as she watches me from the other end of the couch.

I don't know if my expression gives away what I'm thinking, but her eyes change instantly. Her smile evaporates and her features smoke with luscious passion. She switches to that flaming goddess I saw last night.

She adjusts her grip on my feet just a little bit, squeezes up to my thighs, and keeps going.

She slides her hands up....up....up.....and rotates onto all fours to crawl up my body.

Her lips consume me in electric kisses as she lowers her body on top of me. She undulates down me and her breath catches when she feels me getting hard.

She straddles me in her skirt and rotates her hips on me to turn herself on. Her hair spills over my face and her tongue lights me on fire.

I can't keep my hands off her. I grab her hips to grind her down on top of me. Then I scoop up to her breasts.

I snag the knot of her blouse on the way. It falls open like an invitation from Heaven.

I strip up her shirt and dive under her bra. Her big, lush, magnificent breasts fall into my face and mouth. I can't help but devour them.

She squeals and moans while she rides down on me—and then her hand slips between my pants and her saturated underwear.

She starts stroking me through my pants. She turns me on like I can't believe. She's going to make me explode the way she did last night. I don't want that. I want her.

I lean back and push her upright so I can look into her smoldering eyes while I unbutton her shirt.

Her whole body blushes when I peel it back to reveal her gorgeous chest. Her breasts fill my hands and her eyes float half-shut when I squeeze them.

She drags her eyes open and gulps when she starts unbuttoning my shirt. She's undressing me. We're going to do this.

She strokes my bare chest when she pushes my shirt and jacket aside. She keeps going down to my belt. She isn't stopping and neither am I.

I have to kiss her when she pulls my belt loose and unzips my pants. Her tongue swirls around mine. I gasp into her mouth when she shoves her hand into my shorts and her bare fingers clamp around me .

She would finish me off this way if I wanted her to. She won't go all the way unless I show her that I want her to.

I cup the back of her neck and pull her head around so I can look into her eyes while we kiss. The vast depths of her deep brown pools hypnotize me into a trance.

I pull her up, shove my pants down, and tug her panties aside. I hold her eyes when I ease into her, but she can't maintain eye contact.

She falls apart in plaintive sobs when I stroke into her. Her eyes slip out of focus as her heat and wetness surround me.

I hold her in that position so I can see her giving herself to me. She winces and sobs as her cries escalate with my rhythm.

She doesn't move. She stays there and lets me plow in harder, faster, and stronger.

Her wetness gushes around me. She feels incredible. I don't want this to end.

She keeps whimpering and then yelping until her inner muscles clench around me in a death grip. She screams when I slam in to break those spasms apart.

She thrashes in my arms. I have to hold her with all my strength, but she won't stop screaming and gushing and spasming around my shaft. She roars and shrieks before she collapses onto my chest.

I hold her and kiss her hair. I'm still as hard as a rock, but I don't want to hurt her. I also don't want to use her just to get myself off.

Her hair smells delicious. I get an unbearable flood of emotion when I bury my face in her hair and feel her against my cheek and lips.

She's precious. She's perfect.

She lies there whimpering and moaning for a second. Then something changes and she starts rotating her hips on top of me.

I catch my breath at the intensity of what she's doing. She picks up speed so much faster than I expect her to. I'm not prepared for this.

She doesn't hesitate at all. She launches straight back into it, and this time, she sets her own rhythm.

She starts by grinding and twisting on my shaft to drive me as deep into her as she can get me. Her muscles clench every time she does that.

She whines each time, too, and those noises build with her speed and power.

She doesn't stop until she slams herself back on me. She can't get enough thrust from this position. She pushes herself up on her arms and rides me hard.

I stare up at her as she carries me with her into the stratosphere. I can't stop her and I don't want to. I'm falling too fast.

She kisses me hard a few times and then sits all the way up. She bucks her hips, throws back her head, and screams again as her inner channel goes into another convulsion.

I can't hold back. I unload into her and a brutal shockwave of emotion goes off with it. Doing it with her means something different than doing it with every other gold digger out there.

Melody isn't a gold digger. She doesn't have to do it with me at all. She's doing it because she wants it. She wants me.

She topples over me and her delicious mouth envelops me. I feel myself starting to lose it when she kisses me succulently, tenderly, lusciously.

She doesn't kiss with any of the torrential passion of a minute ago. Her lips change to such beautiful, sweet petals that it breaks my heart.

No one has ever kissed me like this. She connects to something so much deeper when she kisses me. She really does admire me. She appreciates something she never expressed in words.

I can actually believe her toast now. She's glad she went through this whole ordeal just so she could meet me.

My fingers glide into her hair. I never want this to end. I want to bask in this feeling that someone actually sees me and values me for something other than my money.

She's the only person who sees me that way. I used to think it was Ray, but he proved he wasn't.

She's the only person who has ever seen me that way. She lets her lips trail off of mine with excruciating slowness. She doesn't want it to end, either.

She finally wilts off me, rolls sideways, and stretches out between me and the couch cushions. Her head falls on my shoulder with a satisfied sigh. Her body goes limp.

I don't dare to unwind my arms from around her body. I don't want to lose this. I want to hold onto it for as long as it lasts—because it won't last. This will end. Then what will happen to me?

Chapter 18: Niko

I run my fingers through Melody's hair and listen to her breathing. Her voluptuous body lies draped over me on the couch. I hope she's comfortable and doesn't get cold.

I'm just wondering if she's asleep when she pries her head back and kisses me on the neck right below my ear.

She burrows into me and sends another electric thrill down my body to my insides. She feels unbelievable.

She nuzzles me close for a minute, nips at my earlobe just enough to turn me on, and falls back against the cushion. "We won't grow moss doing that."

Her voice sounds scratchy after we just did it. I find myself laughing, but I can't look at her. I pretend to shut my eyes.

I don't know what to think about what we just did. We started by making out and touching each other. Now we just hooked up.

Should I think anything about it? Does she want to move back home and live apart from me as soon as this honeymoon ends?

I should ask her, but I don't want to spoil the moment. I also don't want her to think I'm pushing for that.

She raises her hand to comb her hair out of her face. Then she caresses her fingertips down my cheek, neck, and chest.

Her touch makes me shiver. She immediately pulls her hand away. "I'm sorry," she murmurs. "I didn't mean anything by it."

"You don't have to be sorry. I like it when you touch me."

Her head shoots up. "You do?"

"Of course. Do you think I do this kind of thing every day?"

"I....I didn't know.....I just thought.....you know....after what happened today......"

I twist around and frown at her. "What do you mean? You thought what after what happened today?"

"After the deal fell through—and my father and Asher robbed you of your fortune......I want you to know that I'll stick by you. I want to support you while you rebuild. I know my father ruined you the first time and I'm not going to let it happen a second time. We can have a real marriage while you work your way back up. I'm sure you can do it and I want to be part of that. I don't care about the money."

I blink at her in disbelief. "Wait a minute. You....what?"

Now it's her turn to stare at me. "My father and Asher......they bypassed you......they moved to Global Trucking to cut you out of the deal. They're making it out that you didn't give them a competitive rate. They're claiming you breached the contract first so it's okay if they breach it. They broke you.....didn't they?"

"Uh.....no......" I have to think about everything she just said. "They told you that they broke me?"

She shoots off the couch. "They didn't?! They didn't destroy your business?! They didn't ruin you?!"

"No," I murmur. "Nothing like that. I think I would know if they did."

"But....." She looks everywhere. She still lies against me half-naked.

"Is that why you did it with me just now—because you thought I was broke?"

"NO!!" she shrieks and clamps her eyes shut to pull herself together. "I thought.....I don't want it to be like it was last time with your fiancé......I mean.....I thought......."

I have to touch her beautiful face. I understand now. "I'm touched that you think that way about me."

She barely hears me. "Are you telling me......?" She breaks off again. I can just see the wheels turning in her head.

She sits all the way up and covers her eyes. "Oh, my God!" she groans. "You must think I'm totally pathetic."

"Not at all. I think you're incredibly sweet. You made me dinner because you thought I couldn't afford room service. Tonight was one of the best dates I've ever had."

She shudders and looks around. Does she even realize she's still naked?

"I'm sorry," she moans. "I know you don't feel that way about me....."

I cup her chin and make her look at me. "Tell me the truth. Were you serious that you want something real with me?"

She clamps her eyes shut, rallies her courage, and then opens them to lock on me with eerie power. "Yes," she declares. "I do. I understand if you don't, but if you do want to, I'm all in. I'll go the distance with you, for better or for worse or richer or poorer. I'll make good on that vow......if you want to."

I rear off the couch to kiss her. She's immaculate.

I fall back onto the cushion so I can see her. "It means everything that you feel that way about me. I'm not ready to jump into the deep end like that, but I would if you keep proving yourself the way you have been. Nothing is off the table as far as I'm concerned."

"Whatever it is you need from me, I'll do it," she declares. "Even if what you need is time."

I pull her down on me. "You have proven yourself a thousand times. I know you'll keep doing it. If you really mean it, then I don't see any reason why it won't happen exactly the way you say."

She touches my cheek again. "I meant what I said. Meeting you......it's one of the best things that has ever happened to me."

I have to gulp before I can answer her. "I feel the same way about you. We have some time left in this suite. Let's see what happens in that time. If we both still feel that way after the honeymoon, we'll leave together and take it to the next level."

She bursts into a smile of pure relief. She really means it. It's written all over her face.

She sinks back on the couch with another sigh. She would leave it there the way I said.

I can't do that. Something changed tonight—something that will never go back to the way it was before.

Her body breathes with so much possibility. I want her again. I roll on top of her and spiral my hips between her legs.

Her eyes widen and she looks straight up at me when I plunge in again. She doesn't look away as her breath shortens and her pupils dilate.

I dive all the way down into the depths of those eyes. She hides from me. She lays it all on the line and gives me her whole being.

She's real. She's there for me in ways no one ever has been. I want this. I want it to work.

She went through all of this because she thought I had no money. She wants it all with me even if I'm broke.

She would have gone through all of that just to support me and stick by me. What in the world did I ever do to deserve this woman?

Her body unfolds for me in mysterious ways, but it's her pure heart that really wrings the emotions from my soul. I'm touching something so pure I almost tremble to take her. Am I really ready for this?

I'm not, but it sure looks like we're going there.

If she's right, then this could be the best thing that ever happens to me. She's a prize. She's a jewel—and she's mine for the taking. I just have to stay the course and accept the gift she's giving me.

Chapter 19: Melody

I roll over in bed—and then snap alert when I hear a door shut. Niko comes out of the bathroom in my bedroom.

I look around before I remember why he's in my room. He spent the night here—with me.

I collapse back on the pillows as all the memories come rushing back. I did it with him—many times.

He's the best lover I've ever had and I don't even know if we have a relationship. Last night might have just been the greatest night of sex I ever had. That's all it might ever be.

He comes out of the bathroom with his hair wet. He's wearing his suit pants, belt, and nothing else.

He sits down on the mattress next to me, kisses me, and takes my hand. "Don't tell me you regret anything we did last night."

"I don't regret any of it—and I don't regret anything I said last night, either. I will never regret it no matter what happens between us."

He looks away just for a second. "Thank you. I don't know how to thank you enough."

I push myself up. "I need to get up. I need to go see Daddy and Asher. They lied to me. I need to straighten this whole thing out."

"Don't." He pushes me back. "Play along with their game. Don't say anything."

"Play along?!" I fire back. "They used me to screw you over! I'm not going to play along with that!"

"They didn't screw me over, sweetheart. They didn't do anything to me. They tried to, but they didn't. I know they used you and I know they hurt you real bad. I'm just asking you to give me a chance to make it right."

"How? My father still has access to our joint bank account. I don't want him using the account to take your money."

"Please just trust me, baby. It will work better this way. You don't have anything to worry about as far as the deal goes."

I snort. "I wish I could believe that."

"I just have to sew up all the loose ends. I have to seal all the holes in this deal. First it was Ray. Now it's Asher and then your father."

I spin around. "Ray! What about him?"

"He's out. He's gone. He's finished."

I gasp in horror. "What?! When did this happen?!"

"Yesterday. I thought that's what you meant when you asked if anything important happened."

I gape at him with my jaw on the floor. "You got rid of your own brother?!"

"I got rid of a viper who never hesitated to screw me over. He tried to destroy the deal first. He tried to cut out Dante and your father, but I got to Ray first. He's out with nothing. He won't come back."

I gulp hard. "I can't believe this!"

"Now I have to deal with your side of the family. Please trust me, baby. Don't do anything." He kisses me and winds up blushing. "If you want to keep playing along that I'm broke and can't afford room service, you can cook me dinner again. I really loved that."

I try not to smirk at him. "Nice one. You really know how to make your case, don't you?"

"I can't wait to come home tonight to see what you make for me." He kisses me again and stands up. "I expect the house to be spotless and the kids fed when I come home."

I snort with laughter. He grins at me while he finishes getting dressed.

Now I can see his body more clearly in the light of day. His suit hides how ripped he is. Does he even have to try to be the hottest guy in town?

I don't feel like lying in bed, so I get up, take a shower, and make him breakfast before he leaves. He pulls me between his knees on the stool at the kitchen counter. We kiss for a long time before he finally tears himself away.

I know he was only joking, but I spend a long time cleaning up the suite. I pack up all the wedding presents, finish my thank-you cards, mail them out, and spend a bunch of time going through the kitchen to decide what I'm going to make for dinner tonight.

I'm standing there with my head in the pantry when the door lock beeps and clicks open. I freeze for a minute thinking it might be an intruder.

I gasp when I see Niko. "You said you wouldn't come home until tonight! What happened? Is anything wrong?"

"Nothing is wrong. I'm on my lunch break." He comes over to kiss me. Then he looks around. "The place looks great."

"Aren't you going to eat lunch? I could make you something. You don't want to go through the rest of the workday hungry."

"I am hungry, but not for lunch." He comes up to me and pushes me back against the kitchen cabinets.

He dives in and kisses me hard and fast. His mouth snatches my breath away and his tongue slithers into my mouth.

A jet of adrenaline tightens my insides, but he doesn't stop. His hands rake down my sides and he grabs my thigh to pull my leg around him.

His whole body tightens. He's more than hungry. He's ravenous.

He tears off my mouth, jams his forehead against mine, and rasps through bared teeth like an animal. His eyes smolder with buried fire. He looks so unbelievably hot like this.

His hands range all over me. He grabs, kneads, massages, pinches, and squeezes until I moan and whine in his face.

"Come on, baby," he husks. "Come on."

"Niko......" I sob.

"Do you want that, baby?" He screws his pelvis between my legs so I feel how hard he is. All his muscles strain under his suit. "Say you want that. Say you want to bend over for me."

"Niko.....please......"

He drills into my swollen tissues again and makes me squeal in maddening desire. He left me ragged last night from making me climax all night long. Now I respond to him so much faster.

He pulls back, spins me around, and pushes me face down on the counter. He plasters himself against me from behind and drives his hips into my ass.

"You want to take it like that?" he snarls in my ear. "You want me to own this and make you scream?"

I really do scream when he plunges his hand down the front of my pants, stabs his fingers into me from the front, and keeps pumping into me from behind.

He feels how wet I am. His fingers excite me to new heights and I start to climax. I can't stop myself from responding to him.

He doesn't stop fingering me when he strips my pants down and pulls my bare ass toward him. I'm too out of my mind to see what he's doing—until the moment when he flexes his knees and slides in from below.

His fingers spread just enough to let him in. Then he starts rubbing my clitoris while he nails me from behind.

I can't stop tumbling in a maelstrom of explosive climaxes. His shaft fills me to the breaking point, excites every electric node of pleasure inside me, and the deep satisfying thump of his hips against my ass spirals me out of my mind.

I struggle to steady myself by pushing my arms against the cabinets, but he controls all my movements.

I'm still fighting to cope with all these volcanic feelings when he grabs me by the hair, pulls me back to arch into his thrusts, and his scorching breath sears my brain right next to my ear.

"Yeah, baby," he pants with each stroke. "Oh, yeah. That is so damn good. Come on. Give me that. Oh, hell yeah."

I love the strained, tortured break in his voice when he talks like that. He turns me on so much when he takes me like this. I ache for more and more and more without end.

He angles his hips just an inch farther down. His spanking thrusts spatter my wet juices all over my ass and his thighs. That slick of wetness between us feels mind-blowingly erotic.

This encounter is so much hotter for being spontaneous and animalistic. I want him to keep taking me like this—but it wouldn't be spontaneous if he did.

He drives into me, slams me hard against the counter, and roars as he releases into my boiling-hot channel.

I scream again when I feel him spasming. His furious bellows turn to growls and he sinks his teeth into my neck before he crawls up to my ear.

"So good....." he husks. "So good....."

I teeter through another series of orgasms as he pumps the last of his essence into me. He leaves my channel quivering with pleasure—and torturous desire. I don't want to stop, but he has to go back to work soon.

Is he going to eat lunch at all? He'll tell me if he wants to.

He pulls all the way off, spins me around, pins me under his weight again, and kisses me for the ages.

His dripping wet prick brushes my enflamed tissues. I could take him again right now. He drives me wild with how hot he is.

He lets me wrap my arms around his neck while he squeezes my breasts through my shirt. Then he slides his hand between my legs and swirls his fingers in my wetness until he hears me moan for him.

I can never get enough of him, but he pulls away all too soon. He won't stop giving me quick little kisses while he eases off.

His eyes don't soften at all. "That was delicious. I could eat you for lunch every day."

I feel my cheeks burning from the way he's looking at me. "You would get awfully hungry."

He bites back a grin. "I'll pick up something on my way back to the office."

"Are you sure you don't want me to make you something?"

"I don't have time. I just came back for that." He dives in and kisses me again. "I better go before I start doing it again." He backs away. "I'll miss you until I see you again tonight."

He walks out without waiting for me to say goodbye. Now I have to pull myself together so I can go back to thinking clearly.

I could crawl back into bed and fantasize about him for the rest of the day. He arouses so many wicked ideas about all the things we could do together.

I shouldn't be thinking about a guy like that when we aren't even really together. This marriage is still fake.

So we hooked up a few times. That doesn't really change anything. I need to remember that before I sink over my head into something I can't get out of—as if I'm not already.

Chapter 2O: Melody

Niko and I step out onto the balcony overlooking the ballroom in my father's mansion.

"How much longer do we have to keep doing this?" I mutter. "Hasn't the press seen us enough already?"

"Dante wants to keep milking the publicity for as long as it lasts," Niko murmurs under his breath. "I don't think he has too many more of these planned—but look. There are just as many reporters here this time as there were last time."

I groan. "Don't they have anything better to do than recycle yesterday's news?"

He chuckles. "Apparently not. Come on. Let's get it over with so I can take you back to the hotel."

I glance up at him and blush dark red when I see the way he's looking at me. We hooked up the first time after one of these publicity galas.

Niko and I have been doing it non-stop since this whole thing started. I don't have to wonder what he plans to do when he takes me back to the hotel.

I've also been cooking, cleaning, and handling other chores for him while he goes to work. It actually feels like we're really married—which I guess we are.

I keep my hand on his arm while we make our first appearance for the press. We both smile a lot more genuinely now. It's easier to feel enthusiastic, now that Niko and I are getting along so well.

The press finally backs off once they get enough pictures and ask enough questions. It is also getting easier to answer their questions about where we're staying and what we're doing on our honeymoon.

The press already knows that Niko still goes to work every day. That's the whole point of the deal.

He splits off to go get us drinks and snacks. I wander around talking to random people I don't care about.

I really look forward to going back to the hotel with Niko. I don't even care if we just sit on the couch watching movies or anything else.

Hanging out with him is the most enjoyable thing I can think to do right now. I don't want to be anywhere else—especially not here.

I run out of people to talk to, so I migrate over to where my father and Asher are talking to Dante.

My father gives a cruel laugh just as I'm pulling up to listen to their conversation. "Global Trucking might be more expensive, but it will be worth it in the end. I told you Niko couldn't hack it. We should have gone with Global in the first place. Then Melody wouldn't be stuck in this fake marriage. I'm going to dissolve it as soon as Global takes over our transportation and fulfilment. I don't know what Niko will do. He'll have to start liquidating his assets to balance his books."

Dante frowns at him. "What are you talking about? Since when is Niko out of the deal?"

"I just told you," my father replies. "He failed to honor his end of the contract, so we found another carrier to handle fulfillment. He's out. He's done. He's finished. He isn't a billionaire anymore. He isn't even in business anymore. He's nobody." My father laughs again and rubs his hands in sadistic glee. "I wish I could have been there to see his face when he found out."

Dante won't stop furrowing his brow in confusion. "You cut Holloway Industrial so you could pay more to use Global Trucking instead? Is that really what you're telling me?"

"Yes!" My father bursts out in excited laughter. "You never should have trusted that kid, Dante. He's a punk. He's too young and impulsive to be a decent businessman. Maybe he'll learn something in twenty or thirty years, but he can't play with the big boys now."

"I'm afraid you're the one who is too impulsive to be a decent businessman," Dante replies. "Holloway Industrial owns Global Trucking. Didn't you know? He's still running this deal—and now you're going to be paying him even more to do the same job." He shakes his head and turns away. "I never should have partnered with you, Saul. I should have listened to him from the beginning."

"Hey!" my father blurts out. "You can't blame me for trying to protect myself! I had no reason to trust him."

"No reason except a legally binding contract. You should have checked. You only had to do your due diligence on Global to find out that Holloway Industrial was its parent company. Any decent businessman would have done that." Dante looks back and forth between my father and Asher. "I can't believe this. I can't believe I actually let you rope me into this."

He walks off into the crowd and heads straight for the drinks table where Niko is still getting champagne flutes for us.

I can just imagine what Dante will say to Niko about this. Niko has every right to crow over my father's misfortune.

Niko outmaneuvered both him and Asher. They tried to screw him over, but he boxed them in at every turn. They can't get away from him no matter what they do.

I would like to think *they'll* learn something in the next twenty or thirty years. That will never happen.

My father is too old already. He would have learned long ago how to play with the big boys if he was going to learn at all.

Asher will never learn. He doesn't have Niko's brains, insight, or determination. Niko is in another league.

Niko is so far out of Asher's league that Asher doesn't even see the difference. He doesn't know what he doesn't know.

He doesn't recognize how Niko is different. Asher still thinks he and my father can outmaneuver Niko when they don't even know what moves he's making.

My father turns to me as soon as Dante passes out of earshot. "Don't worry, sweetheart. We'll still find a way to get you out of this marriage. I don't want you anywhere near that son of a bitch."

"You should have thought of that before you went through with this marriage," I tell him.

He spins around and his eyes widen. "What's the matter with you? You were the one who wanted to get out of it so bad."

"I never wanted to get into it in the first place, Daddy!" I hear myself snapping at him, but I don't even try to soften my tone. "I only did it because you said you needed the money. Do you even realize how creepy that is—that you sold your only daughter for a business transaction?"

He shuts his mouth and gulps. "It wasn't like that."

"I know what you did to Niko during the first deal, Daddy. I know you were the one who screwed him over. You ruined him and left him penniless. Now you just can't stand to see him back on top. He's even doing better than you are. Don't deny it. I know you did it."

He tries to shrug and winds up squirming. "That was nothing. Everybody does it."

"No, they don't, Daddy!" I snap. "No one does it except dirty, rotten, criminal manipulators like you and Asher. You tried to screw him over a second time, but he saw straight through you. You're getting exactly what you deserve. Everything he said about you is turning out to be right. You're in debt over your head. You aren't good enough to be in business with someone like him or Dante. You'll ruin yourself. All Niko has to do is stand back and watch you fall."

"I never did anything to him!" My father flinches in front of me. "Not anything anyone could prove, at least—so it doesn't count."

I gasp in exasperation and roll my eyes to Heaven. "You're the worst, Daddy. I can't believe I actually tried to help you get away with something like this."

"Where are you going?!" he calls after me. "I meant what I said! We can get you out of this marriage. You don't have to stay with him."

"You could get me out of the marriage how?" I counter. "I agreed to this so you and Niko could use a joint bank account. Anyway, I'm not leaving him. He's a better man than you and Asher put together. I don't care what you do. I'll never sell out Niko again—so don't ask me to. I'm leaving. You can explain to the press that I'm not feeling very well."

I storm across the ballroom, give Niko the briefest excuse, and walk out. Fortunately, there aren't enough reporters around to notice.

I get into the limo and head back to the hotel. I can't be in the same room with underhanded creeps like my father and brother.

I cringe that I'm actually related to them. They're the stupidest, most rotten people I've ever met. How can I share their blood? I'm ashamed even to have the name Gottlieb.

At least Niko understands how I feel about them. I'll just have to explain myself to him when he comes back.

I don't want to do this anymore—I mean I don't want to do press spots at my father's mansion anymore. Maybe Niko can convince Dante to hold them somewhere else—somewhere I won't see my father and Asher again.

I can't believe I'm actually thinking that about my own family. My father and Asher are the only family I have in the world.

I don't want to think about cutting them out of my life completely, but I'm really starting to think that might be for the best.

I'll have to do it if anything real develops between me and Niko. I'll have to choose—and I already have. There's no question who is the better man here.

I march straight into my bedroom, take off my ball gown, and change into my pajamas. Niko can peel them off just as easily when he comes back.

I feel bad about leaving him there to explain things to the press in my place, but to hell with it. My father and Asher make me so mad.

How dare my father justify what he did? He's been lying about it for years, so he must already understand that what he did was wrong.

He hasn't just been lying to me. He lied to everyone at The Billionaires' Club and all his other business associates.

Dante Helme never would have agreed to this business deal if he knew the truth about what my father did to Niko.

Should I tell Dante? Should I tell everyone? Should I actually be the one who destroys my father's reputation and drives him out of business?

That's what I would be doing if I told anyone, especially anyone from the club. Dante would then tell everyone else—which is exactly what he should do.

If he should do it, I should do it.

I'll have to ask Niko about this. He'll be able to tell me what I should do. It's his story after all.

I'm just about to go out to the kitchen to find myself some junk food to drown my sorrows when someone knocks on the outer suite door.

I frown to myself putting the pieces together. It can't be Niko. He has a key.

Who else would knock on my door at this hour? It's nine-thirty at night, so it can't be anyone from housekeeping or the hotel management.

I steal a peak through the little peephole and see Asher standing outside. I yank the door open. "What do you want?"

He smiles at me. "Can I come in? I'm your brother. I want to talk to you....." He looks around. "Unless you want to air our dirty family laundry out here where everyone can hear us."

I compress my lips. I don't want to talk to him, but he's right. It wouldn't do to have a conversation like that where anyone can hear u s.

I stand back to let him come inside. He strolls into the living room and looks around. At least I cleaned the place up first.

He surveys the suite on all sides. The door stands open to the bedroom where I spend my nights with Niko, but Asher doesn't know that.

He sees the bed made up not as nicely as if the hotel maids make it.

The door to the other bedroom is closed. He can't see whether Niko is sleeping in there or not.

"You're here," I snap. "Now what do you want to talk to me about?"

"That was quite a speech you gave at the gala. You sure changed your loyalties fast, didn't you?"

"Loyalties—to what? Daddy has been lying all these years about Niko screwing him over when Daddy was the one who did it in the first place. He lied to get Dante to go in on this deal. This whole fake marriage is based on a lie—for money. Daddy traded me for a bunch of money he probably won't even get—so don't start defending him."

"I'm not defending him."

I turn my back on my brother. "You shouldn't even be here. You tried to ruin Niko, too, by pulling that whole Global Trucking switcheroo."

He follows me into the kitchen. "Did you mean what you said earlier?"

"Which part? If you mean the part about you and Daddy being the worst businessmen alive, then yes, I meant it."

"I mean the part about you not leaving Niko and never selling him out again. Did you mean that?"

"Of course I meant it," I reply over my shoulder and start fishing around in the freezer for whatever is left in the ice cream carton. "You and Daddy deserve everything you get."

I don't know what hits me when a heavy blow strikes me across the back of the head. I never would have believed my own brother could do something like this to me, but it's all really happening.

I struggle to stay upright, but my knees turn to water underneath me. I buckle onto the floor and black out.

Chapter 21: Niko

I get butterflies in my stomach when I pass my key card in front of the lock to open the honeymoon suite. I can just imagine how Melody is waiting for me to come back.

Is she lying naked in bed all warm and wet and soft and welcoming? Is she curled up on the couch in her pajamas with a big smile on her face?

Either way would be good. I get excited thinking about both. She's so much softer and warmer now than she was before. I know she'll be happy to see me.

Maybe now I'll get some answers about why she left the gala when she did.

I walk into the suite and put my keys, phone, and wallet on the kitchen counter. The place sounds too quiet.

"Melody?" I walk into the bedroom. She isn't in there.

I get a bad feeling about this when I return to the living room. I raise my voice a little louder. "Melody! Where are you?"

Nothing.

I search the whole suite. She isn't here.

I make another more detailed search and find her ball gown draped over a chair in the bedroom. She changed. All her clothes are still in the closet.

Did something happen? Did she leave me to go running back to her father—or did her father say something to her at the gala to make her leave?

She said when she left that she was going back to the hotel. Did she? Did she come back here at all? She could have just stayed at her father's house if she wanted to dump me.

My temper flares. She better not have been stringing me along all this time. She better not have spun me a line about having something real with me only to drop me when it suited her.

Did she find out about the Global Trucking situation? Was she playing me until her father and brother could pull the rug out from under me? Is that why she bailed now of all times?

Thinking that ignites my fury. I'm going to find her one way or the other. She better have a damn good explanation for this.

Leading her father and brother around by the nose is one thing. She better not be messing with me. No way will I put up with that.

I call the limo back and fume all the way back to the Gottliebs' mansion. The gala is still going on with Saul holding court with all his glorious admirers.

I storm in and pull him aside so I can get in his face. "Where's Melody?!" I snap. "Is she here?"

His eyes pop. "What?! She said she was going back to the hotel!"

"She isn't there. I searched the whole place. How do I know this isn't another one of your lies?"

"She said she was going to stay with you! She defended you, you stupid prick! She found out about the first deal and she turned against me—against *me!* You're too stupid for a woman like her?"

"Where the hell is she, Saul?!!" I have to fight my voice under control so I don't bellow at him for the whole house to hear. "I want to see her! I want to hear it from her!"

"Will you unplug your ears and listen, you son of a bitch?! She left to go be with you! She isn't here!"

I glare at him. "You better not be lying."

He suddenly frowns at me. "What do you mean—she isn't there?"

"Am I speaking Chinese here?! She isn't at the hotel!"

"Then where is she?"

"How the hell should I know?!" I spin away. "Something must have happened. I gotta find her."

"Hey!" He hustles after me. "I'm coming with you."

"Leave me alone!" I bark over my shoulder. "You've done enough damage to my life already."

"She's my daughter, you piece of shit!"

I round on him spitting tacks. "Well, you sure as hell don't treat her like one, do you? You threw her away for nothing! For all I know, you're the one who convinced her to run out on me. You could be lying to my face right now when she's upstairs laughing at me behind my back."

"I'll prove it to you!" he fires back. "I'll prove to you that she left me to be with you. Will that drive some sense into that block head of yours?"

I don't want to listen to him, but I have to. "Fine. What are you doing to do?"

"Follow me. I'll show you security camera footage of what she said before she left."

He walks off in the other direction. I don't want to go anywhere with this scumbag, but I have to find Melody. I have to hear it from her if she's dumping me or what.

He leads the way to a small room on the mansion's second floor. Three security technicians work in there monitoring dozens of cameras all over the Gottlieb estate.

Saul gives orders and they pull up the confrontation between Melody, Saul, and Asher.

I'm not leaving him. He's a better man than you and Asher put together. I don't care what you do. I'll never sell out Niko again—so don't ask me to. I'm leaving. You can explain to the press that I feel sick.

She actually said those words. She defended me.

The technicians also show footage of her getting into the limo and giving the driver instructions to take her back to the hotel.

"So where is she?" I demand as soon as the footage ends. "She isn't here and she isn't at the hotel."

"Maybe someone at the hotel knows something."

I don't want to listen to a word he says. I pretend not to see him following me out to my car and getting into the back with me on the way back to the hotel.

We get out, go upstairs, search the whole suite another three times, and come up with the same results.

We finally meet up in the lobby where I talk to the clerk behind the desk. "Did Miss Gottlieb say anything about leaving the hotel?" I ask. "We aren't scheduled to check out for another two weeks."

"Miss Gottlieb didn't, but Mr. Gottlieb did," the clerk tells us.

"What?!" Saul exclaims. "I never said anything about her checking out! That's preposterous!"

"Not you, Sir," the clerk replies. "I mean Mr. Gottlieb Junior—Miss Gottlieb's brother. He was here before and said she would be leaving to spend some time with family on Long Island."

I swallow hard. "She....what?"

"She didn't say it, Sir," the clerk replies. "I never saw her. He was the one who said. Mr. Gottlieb was very specific when he mentioned that you would be staying in the suite for the rest of your reservation."

I blink at him as all that random information comes together in my mind. Melody—left with Asher.....Why?

I shake those thoughts out of my head. "So you never saw her—not even once?"

He shakes his head. "No, Sir."

"She didn't come down here? She didn't walk out of the lobby on her own two feet?"

"No, Sir. If she isn't in the suite, then she must have left another way."

I can't help but glance over at Saul.

"He took her to Shadow Glen," he mutters.

"What's that?" I ask.

"It's my other residence on Long Island. He must have taken her there."

"But why? All her clothes are still in the suite." Then I remember. "Her pajamas."

Saul looks up. "What?"

"Her pajamas are gone! She must have changed into her pajamas when she came home from the gala. She was wearing her pajamas!"

He frowns at me. "What does that have to do with anything?"

"He took her by force! Don't you see?" I spin away. "I gotta find her. Send me the address for the estate. I'm going to get her."

"Hey!" Saul yells after me. "We have to call the Police!"

"You do it!" I call over my shoulder. "I don't have time to stand around."

I hustle outside and get back into my limo. I don't wait for Saul to send me the address.

It doesn't take me long to pull up the location for Shadow Glen Estates. It's a big, sprawling property way out at the far end of Long Island. No wonder Asher took Melody there.

It's a long ride out there. It gives me plenty of time to think of all the gory ways I'm going to make Asher suffer for this.

He better not have hurt her. I'll cut him up into small pieces and feed him to the fish in the East River if he harmed a single hair on her head.

Chapter 22: Melody

I swim back to consciousness and groan when I feel the lump on the back of my head. I only have to look around to see where I am.

I'm lying on the enormous sleigh bed in one of the upstairs bedrooms at Shadow Glen Estates on Long Island. The sky is just getting light outside. I must have been here all night—or most of it.

My disastrous encounter with Asher comes back to haunt me. He knocked me out and brought me here for some reason.

Whatever it is can't be anything good. He's been up to no good for so long. I don't even know if he's capable of anything good anymore.

I never dreamed he would actually go so far as to knock me out and kidnap me just to keep me away from Niko.

Asher better not start giving me a bunch of lame excuses like saying I don't know what's good for me and I'm too smitten to think straight when it comes to Niko.

I hate to admit it, but that is exactly the kind of thing Asher would say. Asher and my father have treated me so disrespectfully lately. I wouldn't put this past them, either.

I climb off the bed and pat myself down. I'm still wearing my pajamas—and I don't have my phone.

I didn't have it on me when Asher showed up at the honeymoon suit. My phone was in my purse—the little clutch I took to the gala.

Did he leave it in the suite? Will Niko find my phone and realize I didn't leave the suite by choice?

I sure hope he doesn't think I ran out on him. I can't call him anyway. I can't call anyone to tell them where I am or that I'm in trouble.

I don't even know if I am in trouble. I might be perfectly safe here—except that Asher won't let me leave. I don't even have to ask him to know that. He wouldn't have brought me here against my will if he ever planned to let me go.

I go over to the window. It's forty feet off the ground, but I might be able to climb down. Then I could run for it.

I just need a phone. I can call 911—or I can call Niko—or something. I have to get off the property.

The good news is that I know exactly where I am. I know how to get back to Manhattan. I just don't know how to find Niko after that.

I know how to get back to my father's mansion, but I won't go there. I don't trust that my father isn't involved in this.

I'm just studying the window frame when the bedroom door opens without anyone knocking first.

I stiffen when Asher walks in holding a tray covered by a silver dome. He is not trying to be nice to me. The snake.

"What the hell are you trying to pull, Asher?" I snap. "You kidnapped me!"

He puts the tray down on the table by the bed. "I was trying to protect you. You know you can't stay with Niko Holloway. That's nonsense."

"What I do is none of your business! You and Daddy married me to him. I didn't want that. You did!"

He clucks his tongue and shakes his head. "You weren't supposed to fall for him. That just proves how brainless you are. Now eat your breakfast. You need to stay healthy."

"Like you care," I snarl. "Where's Daddy? He better not be behind this."

"He isn't here, so he can't help you. He's still in Manhattan. I'll call him later to tell him you're okay. You have nothing to worry about."

I narrow my eyes at him. My father is in Manhattan. Asher took me to Long Island.

Asher should have taken me to my father's mansion if he really wanted to protect me. Asher *would* have taken me to my father's house if my father was in any way involved in this.

My father doesn't know about this. Asher kidnapped me on his own with no help from anyone. The only question is why.

I don't trust him to tell me the truth. I don't trust him to do anything.

He sees me hesitate and nods down at the tray again. "Eat your breakfast. You'll find some clothes in the closet over there. Get dressed. You can walk around the house, but you can't go outside until we work this thing out."

"Work what out?"

He walks away to the door. "We'll talk about it later. Don't do anything stupid. You're in enough trouble already."

He leaves and shuts the door behind him. Now I'm all alone with a breakfast tray.

I don't want to accept anything he's giving me, but I guess I have no choice.

He's right that I need to keep my strength up. I don't want to get caught unprepared if I find a chance to escape from here.

What does he need to work out? How does my presence here accomplish anything for him? I don't get it.

I sigh in defeat, sit down next to the tray, and take the lid off. I find a bowl of cereal, a small jug of milk, and a cut-up apple.

I snort at the food. I should have known Asher wouldn't treat me like any honored guest. I'm his prisoner, so of course he's going to feed me like one.

I pour the milk into the cereal, eat it, and then finish off the apple. Now I have the whole day to spend how I want—except that I can't spend the time with Niko.

This room doesn't have a TV or a streaming service, either. I'm alone with no access to the internet or the outside world.

I find all the clothes I need in the closet. I keep my outfit casual with jeans, a short-cropped T-shirt, and a short, suede blazer over the top.

I don't find any shoes other than heels, so I stay barefoot. I have to be prepared for anything, including running, climbing, or anything else I might have to do.

I spend the rest of the day searching the house. All the servants are still here and working—and so is a whole team of armed security guards.

They patrol the grounds and stand in front of every entrance. I don't try to go outside to see what they'll do to stop me.

What did Asher tell them about me? He might have told them that I'm in danger and they have to keep me in the house for my own protection. That would be just like Asher.

I'm just going back to my room at the end of the day when one of the housemaids comes up to me at the door.

She holds out a black garment bag. "Mr. Gottlieb would like you to wear this when you come downstairs for dinner, Miss."

"Mr. Gottlieb who?" I ask. "Is my father here?"

"No, Miss. I meant Mr. Gottlieb Junior. He's in charge here this weekend."

I snort and push the garment bag back into her hands. "Go tell him I'm not going to dress up for him. Tell him to send me a pair of prison overalls and be done with it."

I walk into my room and slam the door behind me just to make my point. How dare Asher try to dress this up as something it isn't? How dare he try to treat me as a guest when he's holding me as a prisoner in my own house?

I'm still sitting there seething in fury when he strolls in without knocking again. "Don't you ever knock?" I snap. "Didn't anyone ever teach you any manners? Oh, what am I saying?! I know they didn't."

"You wouldn't have invited me if I knocked. Would you?"

"Of course not! I don't want to see you, Asher. I don't want to have anything to do with you."

"Then I guess you don't want to eat dinner. I came to invite you to join me."

I turn my head to one side so I don't have to see him. "I'll eat up here."

"You won't eat up here. You can come downstairs and with me or you won't eat at all. We can play hardball if you really want to."

I snort and get to my feet—not because I'm so desperate for food. I want to see if I can spot any vulnerabilities in this place. There has to be something.

He grins in triumph when he leads the way back out into the corridor. He walks extra slowly down the landing to the stairs. He acts like we have all the time in the world to enjoy each other's company.

"Don't worry," he tells me. "You won't be trapped here forever."

"At least you're admitting now that I am trapped. That's a step in the right direction."

"Just try to appreciate this time for what it is. It won't last. Then everything will be perfect."

"What's your version of perfect?"

"When we take over the deal from Niko and Dante, of course—when Daddy and I take control of the whole marketplace. Don't worry. It won't take that long. I have almost the whole system in place already."

I do a double-take and almost give myself whiplash when I spin around. "You're trying to ruin Dante, too, now? Are you out of your mind?!"

Asher faces front. "Dante isn't all that. He's just a guy. What's your problem? This is just business. It isn't like you know how it works. You're clueless."

I shake my head at nothing, but I know better than to try to reason with him. "You're out of your mind. I sure hope Daddy isn't in on this."

"He isn't, but he'll benefit from it when my plans come through."

"Like your plan to replace Holloway Industrial with Global Trucking? Are those the plans you mean?"

We get to the grand dining room just then. Asher sits down at the head of the table like he's some kind of goddamn duke or something.

Luckily for me, he seats me at the very far end of the table facing him. I'm as far away from him as I can possibly be without leaving the room.

I find myself studying him from that distance. He's a moron if he thinks he can end-run both Niko and Dante.

Asher and my father working together couldn't touch Niko by himself. Now it's two against one going in the other direction. Asher doesn't stand a chance.

We sit in silence while the staff serves us. Then they retreat.

I find myself watching the servants. They go in and out of the house all day long. I bet they all have phones. I bet even the security guards have phones.

Asher wouldn't be able to ban the staff from carrying phones. Some of them must have families. The staff members need to be contactable while they're working in case something comes up.

Asher leans back in his chair and studies me just as closely while we eat. I tell myself I'm keeping my strength up by eating this food. I'm not doing it to get along with him.

"So what made you fall for that asshole anyway?" Asher asks. "He's the enemy and now you're all sweet on him."

"I fell for him because he isn't you," I snap back. "He's everything you are not. I admire that about him."

He snorts. "I'm your brother. You couldn't fall for me, but let's take Taylor for example. You had a great guy. Now you're running after some sleaze because he has a bigger wallet."

I don't tell Asher about his own plans to ruin Niko. Asher wanted Niko to lose all his money. He would have been penniless if Asher had his way.

"I'm not engaged to Taylor, remember?" I reply. "You and Daddy made sure of that."

"But you still love him. You didn't have to throw him over for some rich cocksucker just because he's taller and better looking."

I don't answer that, either. Asher doesn't need to know about Taylor dumping me.

That's the moment when it hits me. Asher must be jealous of Niko. Niko is everything Asher is not.

Niko is smart, cunning, far-seeing, upright, honest, and steadfast in his determination to accomplish his goals. Asher will never be any of those things.

Niko is also taller and Asher thinks Niko is better looking than Taylor, too. I wouldn't go that far, but Asher thinks so. He's jealous of Niko.

Niko didn't get me to like him by being taller, better-looking, or rich. He got me by being a nice guy who took care of me, protected me, and spoke up for me when I needed it the most.

He was the only one who was there for me after the wedding. He didn't have to be. He could have left me alone in my own misery.

He cares about me more than my own father and brother. Niko shows that in a thousand ways. He deserves my dedication more than anyone else. He deserves it a lot more than Taylor does.

Chapter 23: Melody

Asher tries to act relaxed at his end of the dining table, but I know him too well. I see straight through him.

He doesn't like what's happening to me. I'm waking up to what he really is. He doesn't want me to see that when I look at him.

He would rather keep me as an innocent little girl who doesn't know what a demon she's sitting across the table from.

That doesn't matter because I know now. It doesn't matter if he keeps me locked up in this house. He'll never pull the wool over my eyes again.

I'm still lost in my own thoughts when the servers come back to take our dishes away. They clear away the dinner service and get ready to serve dessert in its place.

I sit back in my chair when one of the male servers bends over to pick up my plate.

That's the moment when I hear his phone buzz in his pants pocket. He has it on mute, so I'm the only person who hears the notification. Asher doesn't hear it. He's too far away.

I freeze to my chair with my fork suspended over my plate. I shake it off and start eating my dessert. I don't want Asher to know anything is going on.

I act as casually as I can to get through the rest of dinner. Asher makes a few more noises from his end of the table to let me know he has Niko and Dante in the palm of his hand. Yeah, right.

Asher walks me back up to my room after dinner. I count down the seconds before he leaves me the hell alone. I don't want to be related to this slimeball for another second.

I finally say a polite, "Good night," and shut the door with him on the outside. Thank God.

I sink onto the bed panting hard and shaking all over. I have to get to a phone no matter what. I don't care what Asher does to me as long as I warn Niko.

Once I do that, I can call 911 and get out of here. Asher can't keep me under surveillance around the clock.

His security people might be able to, though. He has enough of them. He probably won't leave the estate unguarded even for a minute. In fact, I'm certain he won't.

I can't sit still. I pace around the room for what feels like hours. I glance out the windows a few times, but the sight of all the security guys gives me the shakes. I can't look at that.

I wait until eleven-thirty, ease the bedroom door open just a crack, and hold my breath to listen. I'm the only person awake—at least, I hope I am.

I tiptoe out onto the landing and pause there to listen again. Asher said I was free to move around the house at will, so I'm not technically doing anything wrong yet.

Oh, what the hell am I even thinking? He's the one who's doing something wrong. I'm the victim here.

I inch down the stairs and creep do the hall to the kitchens. The dishwashers are still in there. The servers are putting away the food and the chef is closing up the kitchen for the night.

I see the same server from the dining room. He had his phone in his pants pocket, so it's probably still there. I won't be able to use that.

I take a chance and slip into the staff locker room behind the kitchen. This is where the staff changes into their uniforms before they start work.

I go through the room in a frenzy and pat down every single jacket and shirt in sight. None of them has a phone in it—not until I come to the very last one.

It's a black leather jacket with a belt around the waist. I almost drop the phone when I pull it out of the inner pocket.

I scramble to turn the phone on, but I wind up staring at one of those dot pattern security codes. I try a dozen different codes until the phone locks and tells me to enter my password.

I actually blurt out, "Damn it!" before I realize I'm not supposed to be making any noise.

I look around in desperation—and come face to face with the server from the dining room.

He's a young guy with curly black long-cut hair and deep black eyes. He narrows them at me and scowls. "What are you doing? You better not be trying to steal that phone."

"You gotta help me!" I gasp. "Asher is holding me here as a prisoner! I need to call for help! Please....you gotta help me! Just let me make one phone call! You know he brought me here against my will! You can't let him get away with this! I'm begging you! Just one phone call! Don't tell him! This is my only chance!"

The guy frowns at me and then purses his lips before he takes the phone away from me. "Just make it quick. I could lose my job over this."

He enters the code and hands me the phone back.

"Thank you so much!" I gush and attack the phone.

I said one phone call, but I can't bring myself to call 911—not before I warn Niko.

My hands shake when I dial his number. Please Dear God in Heaven let him answer.

It rings once and switches straight to voicemail. Damn it.

My heart pounds while I wait for the message to end. The server guy stands there staring at me while I shuffle my feet in agitation.

The phone finally beeps. "Niko!" I pant. "You have to listen to me! I'm at Shadow Glen Estate on Long Island! Asher brought me here. He knocked me out in the honeymoon suite—and now he's planning something to take down both you and Dante. You have to warn Dante. Asher won't even tell me what he's planning—probably because I warned you last time. Don't worry about me! Just protect yourself! I'll try to find a way to get out of here as quickly as I can. I hope you're all right. Bye."

I hang up and stare at the phone. Now I have to call 911. I don't even know how long I have left before I have to go back upstairs.

I don't dare to glance at the server guy. Is he about to take the phone away from me?

I raise my finger to dial the number when we hear voices out in the kitchen.

The server grabs the phone out of my hands and pushes me away. "Mr. Gottlieb is coming! Quick—go that way and get out of here!"

The server pushes me down a different hall toward the bathrooms. I don't even have time to thank him before he walks back to the kitchen. Asher's voice fires back and forth with the kitchen staff.

I race down the hall to the bathroom, and from there, I duck out into the butler's pantry. I can slip through the dining room and up the stairs while Asher is occupied in the kitchen.

I get through the dining room, but when I make it as far as the main entrance foyer to the house, I see the front door standing open.

A bunch of security guys stand out there talking to each other. Then they walk away in opposite directions.

They leave the door unguarded. This might be my only chance to get away.

I ease over to the door and look out into the night. Solar-powered lights line the driveway leading to the estate's front gate. From there, I can slip away into the neighborhood and hide in the bushes where no one will see me.

I glance left and right, but I don't see any of the security guys. I won't get another chance like this.

I take one step forward when Asher appears out of nowhere, grabs my arm, and yanks me back inside. "Where do you think you're going?!" he snaps.

"Let me go, Asher!" I fight back and try to hit him.

He grabs both my arms, but when I still won't settle down, he hauls off and clubs his fist across the side of my head.

He sends me sprawling across the floor. I would scream in pain and surprise, but that blow leaves me dazed.

I can't move before he pounces on me, grabs me by the back of the shirt with one hand, and clenches his other hand in my hair.

I really do scream when he drags me off the floor and up the stairs. I'm too stunned to stay upright. My knees wobble, but he keeps yanking me upright and forcing me to climb.

"You just had to turn this into a conflict, didn't you?" he barks in my ear. "We could have had a nice, relaxing vacation in the country—but no! You had to make this as unpleasant as possible—just like you always do."

He jerks me onto the landing and pushes me into a different room.

It takes me a second to realize why he's putting me in here instead of that big, fancy guest room where I woke up.

This room doesn't have any windows. Of course not. That would be the very first way I tried to escape.

This room serves as the maids' storage room. It has a small single bed in case one of the maids has to spend the night upstairs for some reason.

Huge shelves cover the other two walls just a few feet away from the bed. Linens, towels, and other household goods stack the shelves. That's the whole room.

He pushes me through the door hard enough to make me sprawl on the floor a second time.

"And stay there this time!" he barks and slams the door.

The lock clicks when he turns the key from the outside. So much for my glorious escape attempt. Now I really am trapped with no way out—but at least Niko knows where I am.

I just hope he cares about me enough to come after me.

Chapter 24: Niko

I can't sit still in the limo all the way to Long Island. Every minute racks my nerves. Is Melody even still alive? Is Asher unhinged enough to harm his own sister?

He's capable of anything. I know that now—and I also know he doesn't care about her. She's a means to an end to him. Everything is a means to an end to him.

The limo pulls into the driveway at Shadow Glen Estates. The chauffeur stops when we see a bunch of heavily armed security men standing at the entrance gate.

These aren't your garden variety security guards making minimum wage to sit around and eat donuts.

These guys wear black business suits with black sunglasses and coiled earpieces in their ears. Every single one of these men is beefy, ripped, and on high alert.

They carry state-of-the-art automatic weapons. Each man scans the surroundings like he knows exactly how to use his weapon.

The chauffeur stops at a safe distance. "We can't get in there," he murmurs through the window. "They got the place under guard."

I don't answer. I get out and stride toward the gate.

Four security guys come toward me holding out their hands. "You can't come in here, Sir," one of them tells me. "This is private property."

"This is not private property!" I wave at the street behind me. "This is a public thoroughfare and I have every right to be here! Now I want to see Melody Gottlieb and I want to see her immediately!"

"We can't do that, Sir," the same guy tells me. "We're holding her here for her own protection. Her life is in danger...."

"Her life is in danger from her brother! He kidnapped her—or did he tell you that her life was in danger from me? At least let me see her alive. If you don't, I'll call the Police to storm this place and all of you will be implicated in kidnapping and false imprisonment. Is that what you want? You guys are all complicit in a crime. Did you know that?"

A few of them shake their heads. Others exchange glances.

That one guy straightens his arm in front of me and pushes me back. "Go back to your car, Sir. Stay over there on public property and I'll call Mr. Gottlieb to straighten this out."

"He can't straighten it out. He's the criminal here. Don't you get that?"

"Step back, Sir!" the guy orders. "Don't make me tell you again!"

The chauffeur must be listening because he gets out of the driver's compartment to back me up.

I step away and return to the car while one of the security guys makes a phone call from the gatehouse.

"Mr. Gottlieb is on his way down," he announces as soon as he hangs up.

"How do you guys even know Melody is even still alive?!" I fire back. "Have any of you seen her alive? Are you really going to stand there and defend a kidnapper and possible murderer?"

None of them answers. Good. Maybe now they'll realize what's really going on here.

I can't stop pacing around with my hands on my hips. I try to squint through the trees toward the giant mansion on the property.

I try to see Melody in any of the windows. I got her message, but it didn't tell me anything I didn't already know.

I didn't know Asher was moving against Dante. I knew Asher was moving against me, but the guy must be truly cracked if he's going after Dante. Dante is Saul's and Asher's meal ticket. Asher must have popped a cylinder if he thinks he can screw Dante.

None of that matters. I have to get Melody back. I didn't think I cared about her this much. Then I lost her.

I can't lose her again. I have to find her before Asher does something terrible to her—if he hasn't already.

I freeze when I see him coming down the driveway in one of his sloppy suits. He thinks he's so suave when he's really just a clown.

He grins when he sees me. What a jackass. He actually thinks me coming here is a joke. He's about to wake up to a rude surprise.

He waves for the security guards to back off, but they don't stop guarding the entrance. The chauffeur is right. We can't get in there—not through the front gate.

Asher smirks at me. "Can I help you?" he asks.

"You can die, you worthless piece of shit."

He clucks his tongue and shakes his head. "You should know better than that. You know, I'm really surprised a Terminator like you fell so hard for my skank sister. She's brainless, you know. She doesn't know anything, but you fell for her, hook, line, and sinker."

I narrow my eyes at him. "You better not have done anything to her or I swear to God...."

"What I do with her is none of your business," he snaps a little more harshly. "You will never see her again. If you try, you'll be the one who gets her in trouble. You'll have no one to blame but yourself for what happens to her."

"You won't get away with this," I mutter.

"I already have. I have Melody. You don't. Now I'll do what I want with her. If you knew what was good for you, you would handle your own business instead of worrying about people and things that don't concern you."

"You can't beat me—in business or in anything else," I fire back. "You're weak and stupid. You better pull your head in before you get hurt."

He shakes his head again and turns away. "We'll see about that. This marriage between you and Melody was never real. You were never going to keep her—and you don't even want her. I don't know why you're acting like you do. She's a piece of meat—that's all. Go back to Manhattan and mind your own business. You'll get further."

He turns his back on me and walks back up the driveway. He passes through the gate and the security guys shut it behind him.

I should be more concerned about letting him have the last word—especially after he said that about Melody.

I don't care about that because I'm going to get her back. A whole army of security guys won't stop me.

A pathetic little worm like Asher Gottlieb definitely won't stop me. I can crush him under my heel. That's exactly what he deserves. I just need to get to him.

I back away and get back into the limo. "Where to, Sir?" the chauffeur asks me.

"Take a drive around the block," I tell him.

His head shoots up. "Sir?"

"Drive around the block." I pull out my phone. "We aren't going anywhere."

He drives around the block. I tell him to park in the shade under some trees around the nearest corner. The security guys can't see me here and no one can see me from Shadow Glen and the house.

I spend ten minutes on my phone and make a few key calls. The guys in The Billionaires' Club joke around with each other by saying I'm a younger Jimmy Hoffa but with better manners. They don't know the half of it.

I run one of the biggest trucking companies in the world. No one can get the job done like we can.

I direct the chauffeur to another shady spot on the other side of the Shadow Glen estate. I get out and tell him to take the car back to Manhattan. I won't need it anymore.

I jog across the street and get into a square, white utility van with a big curlicue bakery logo on the outside.

I open the back doors and climb into the back where I meet up with fifteen hefty truckers all jammed inside. They pull me in and slam the doors so no one sees us.

All these guys are carrying automatic weapons, too. They're all dressed in black with black balaclavas pushed up on their foreheads.

"What are we doing, Mr. Holloway?" one of them asks me. "Who are we here to rescue?"

"There's a big house right over that stone wall over there." I point to the side of the van. "A young lady is being held there against her will and the kidnapper is threatening her life. We're going in to get her out."

The guys all nod. "No problem, Mr. Holloway," a different guy replies. "Just tell us where you want us to go."

"We're going in through the kitchen delivery entrance. We should be able to waltz right in without anyone bothering us." I lean over all of them and yell up to the driver. "Are you ready, Chico?"

"You bet, Mr. Holloway!" he calls back. "I'm ready to roll."

"Let's do it." I sit down with the men in the back. Chico puts the van in gear and drives off around the block.

He's a young kid with shoulder-length black hair. He wears a bakery uniform—because he works for a bakery—a bakery I deliver for. This van belongs to my company and he works for me to deliver the bakery goods.

Shadow Glen Estates is one of his regular stops. I know all kinds of people in all kinds of places that I'm sure Asher Gottlieb doesn't know about.

Chico slides closed the safety door separating the rear compartment from the cab. No one can see me and all these armed men sitting in the back.

The guys get busy pulling down their balaclavas. I don't bother. I don't give a flat shit who sees me. Asher is holding Melody as a prisoner. I don't need to know anything else.

I might not have wanted to marry her in the first place, but I am married to her. No one is going to stand there and call her a piece of meat to my face. Hell no.

The brakes squeak when the van stops. The guys and I all strain our ears to listen when Chico talks to someone else.

The van starts rolling again and Chico calls out, "We're in! Get ready to launch!"

My tension spikes off the charts. Here we go.

The van stops a second time. Chino's driver door slams and then he opens the rear doors from the back. The guys and I unload at a loading dock behind the giant Shadow Glen estate house.

Two big loading bays open into the kitchen. The place is wide open, so no one can accuse us of breaking and entering.

The guys surround me in guns and hold the kitchen staff at gunpoint as we head through the kitchen into the house itself. I better not find Asher in here hurting Melody. He's a dead man if I do.

Chapter 25: Melody

I jump up off the tiny maid's bed when I hear the key turn in the lock. The door swings open. My fright turns to rage when I see Asher standing there.

He doesn't even pretend to smile at me. He stalks into the room, grabs my arm, and yanks me out of the room. "Let's go," he barks. "Don't give me any bullshit."

I yell, "Asher!" but he doesn't let go of me.

He marches me across the landing and down the stairs. At least he doesn't drag me around by the hair this time.

He shoves me down the hall and into the library. It's a big, comfortable room full of couches, chairs, desks, and fireplaces.

I gasp when I discover my father standing there. "Daddy!" I exclaim. "What are you doing here?! You better not be involved in this!"

"I wasn't involved in anything, sweetheart," he tells me. "I was worried when Niko came around saying Asher took you by force. I had to come and see you for myself."

"Asher *did* take me by force. I told you I was going back to Niko. Did you think I changed my mind? I wouldn't have come here if I did. Asher hit me over the back of the head....."

"Don't make it out like it was some kind of violent act," Asher cuts in. "I did it to protect you."

"It was a violent act!" I shoot back. "Do you think hitting someone over the back of the head isn't a violent act?! You're out of your mind—but we already knew that."

"I did it to get you out of that fake marriage. You said you didn't want to do it...."

"I didn't want to do it at first! I told you point blank at the gala that I was going back to him—so don't pull that crap about trying to protect me and trying to get me out of it. You did this for your own selfish gain—so you could pull a fast one on Dante and Niko and push them out of the deal."

Asher shakes his head. "You don't know what you're talking about. You really need to learn to keep your mouth shut about things that don't concern you."

"Do you think my own safety doesn't concern me?!"

My father shakes his head. "That doesn't matter now, sweetheart. You're out of the marriage anyway. You don't have to go back to him. We'll find another way to honor our business contract."

"I'm not out of the marriage. You couldn't put the divorce through without my signature and I would never agree to that. I don't want to be out of it. I'm in love with him. Do you get that—both of you? I'm in love with Niko Holloway—thanks to you two. If I have my way, I'll spend the rest of my life with him, give him everything, and we'll make this a real marriage."

My father gasps. "What are you talking about?! You aren't in love with him! You were engaged to Taylor!"

I groan and roll my eyes. "Oh, will you wake up, Daddy? Taylor and I are long over. You destroyed that relationship, but that's okay because you brought me a much better man. You brought me the man I was supposed to marry—and now I am married to him."

"This is stupid," Asher growls. "I clearly didn't slap enough sense into that fluffy little head of yours. You don't know what's good for you."

"I've been trying to get away from you all this time so I could go back to him! You're the one who doesn't have a single brain cell between your ears. I'm in love with him! I called him first last night—even before I got a chance to call 911. You two are going to crash and burn because he's the better man. I hope I never see either of you again."

My father's eyes widen when he finally realizes what I'm saying. Asher narrows his eyes and glares at me. "You filthy rotten bitch!" Asher snaps. "I knew you were banging him behind closed doors."

"You're jealous and you have every reason to be!" I fire back. "You will never be half the man Niko Holloway is. You'll spend the rest of your life watching him rise while you sink into the gutter where you belong."

He lunges for me impossibly fast, seizes me by the throat, and slams me back against the wall. "You foul-mouthed bitch! Don't you ever talk to me like that again! I'll kill you!"

He raises his hand and belts me across the face again. His other hand clenches around my neck hard enough to suffocate me.

He's holding me hard enough to stop me from breathing. His hand on my neck makes the force of his blow so much worse, but I don't care. I love Niko. The sooner Asher and my father get that through their heads, the better for all of us.

My father rushes over to us and tries to get between me and Asher. "Stop it, son! Leave her alone! This is nothing to get violent over...."

My father tries to pull Asher away from me, but Asher turns on him next. Asher keeps his hand locked around my throat, plants his other hand on my father's chest, and Asher straightens his arm with unbelievable force to shove my father away.

My father pitches onto his back and slides away across the smooth tile floor.

"You stupid old man!" Asher bellows. "Don't you ever try to tell me what to do again! Do you think I give a shit about you or your trifling little business anymore? I cut you out! Do you hear me? I took your goods, cut you out of the business, and used your money to start my own empire. You got nothing now, understand? You're nothing! You're finished! You're done! Everything you had is mine! Don't you ever come near me again or I swear to God I'll kill you!"

My father screams in a combination of horror and heartbreak. The fall must have hurt him worse than Asher is hurting me.

My father twists onto his side trying to get up, collapses, rolls onto his back, and lies there writhing in agony. He looks like he's really hurt.

"Daddy!" I shriek and tear out of Asher's grip to go over there.

Asher doesn't react fast enough. I fall on my knees next to my father, but Asher catches up with me in a split second.

He grabs me by the shoulders, hurls me sideways across the floor, and pulls a gun out of his rear waistband as he stalks toward me to hunt me down.

I flip over onto my seat and back-pedal to get away from him, but I wind up bumping into one of the couches. I can't get away.

He levels the gun at me. Now I'm just as finished as my father.

He lies gasping on his back across the room. What's wrong with him?

Every fiber of my being tells me to go over there and help him, but I can't. Asher blocks me and aims the gun at my head.

I glare up at him. "You'll pay for this," I snarl.

He cracks a grin. "You won't be around to see it. Adios, little sister."

His finger tightens on the trigger grip and a gunshot cracks across the room. I jump out of my skin, but the bullet doesn't hit me.

Asher spins the other way as a dozen armed men storm into the library. They're all wearing black face masks and holding Asher at gunpoint with automatic weapons.

"Don't move, pal!" one of them yells, yanks Asher's gun out of his hands, and they shove him face down on the floor.

Niko hustles up to me and wraps his arms around me. "Are you all right?!" He moves back to see my bruised face. "That son of a bitch!"

I hold onto him and then push him away just as fast. "My father! We have to call an ambulance, Niko! He's in trouble!"

I scramble over to my father. His glazed eyes trace back and forth across the ceiling. He doesn't move in any other way except to open and close his lips in silent words.

Niko gets on his phone and calls 911. The gunmen zip-tie Asher's wrists together behind his back. We all hear him yelling in the background.

Niko has to yell, too, so the operator can hear him. I can't even tell what's wrong with my father.

I clasp his hand. "Hold on, Daddy!" I whimper. "The ambulance is on its way."

"Baby......" he husks.

I choke back tears. I can't lose my father.

Niko comes up behind me and his hand falls on my shoulder. Thank God he's here. He saved me from Asher. Niko saved me from everything.

He'll be the one to get me through this—whatever terrible thing is about to happen next. Niko will always be there. I know that now. He never lets me down.

"I love you, Daddy!" I whimper. "Please don't leave me!"

"I love you more than anything, sweetheart," he rasps. "I let you down.....I did wrong.....I'm sorry......"

A commotion breaks out behind us. I don't get a chance to turn around before Niko wraps his arms around me, lifts me away from my father, and pulls me clear as the paramedics rush in to surround him.

Niko moves in front of me to block my view. "Come on!" he urges. "You're coming with me! We'll follow the ambulance to the hospital! We can't stay here!"

He hustles me out of the room, through the kitchen, and out the back of the house. We make it to the kitchen loading dock just as a limo pulls in behind us. I don't see any security guys anywhere.

Niko pulls open the door for me to get in, climbs in behind me, and the car pulls away.

Two other vehicles sit parked outside the loading dock. One is a white bakery van. The other is the ambulance. It points its nose outward with its back doors open toward the kitchen.

The limo glides down the driveway and sits there idling until the ambulance driver gets behind the wheel, flips on his lights and sirens, and pulls away.

My father is in that ambulance. What will happen to me if he dies?

I can't live with that. I can't face it if this whole disastrous situation ends in his death.

The ambulance swivels out onto the road. The limo angles in behind it just as dozens of cop cars swarm the estate. None of them stop us from leaving.

Now my brother is on his way to jail. That's the least he deserves. I just hope Niko and his men don't get in trouble for saving me.

Chapter 26: Niko

I sit down in the hospital waiting area chairs and hand Melody a bottle of fruit juice. Most people waiting around in hospitals drink way too much coffee. I want her to drink something healthy—or at least healthier.

Saul is still in surgery. He's been in there since the ambulance brought him in. No one comes to tell us what's wrong with him.

Melody doesn't see the juice bottle in her hands. She sits perched on the very edge of her seat staring toward the hall leading to the operating room.

She holds every muscle in her body tense. She never looks at me or softens, not even when I rub her back and run my fingers through her hair. That's okay. I don't need or expect a response.

Her face looks awful. She has too black eyes, a puffy bruised cheek, and a swollen, split fat lip.

Asher must have knocked her around pretty bad, but she doesn't notice that, either. She only cares about her father.

I don't tell her that her father was the one who told me where she was. I wouldn't have gotten to her in time without her father's help.

Saul wasn't the best guy in the world, but he wasn't the worst, either. I guess I gave him a bad rap all these years.

I don't hope he dies. Melody needs him even if he isn't about to win any Father of the Year awards.

I twist the cap off my juice bottle and take a gulp. We've already been sitting here for four hours waiting for some news about Saul.

I keep fielding texts from my guys telling me everything going on at Shadow Glen. All of them have given statements to the Police. Asher is in jail getting interrogated about the kidnapping.

My guys keep warning me that the Police want to question me and Melody. I tell my guys to tell the Police where Melody and I are.

I have nothing to hide, but I sure as hell plan to take care of Melody first. The Police can question me all they like after this nightmare is over.

I also field a metric crap ton of emails and frantic texts from Dante, all his people, Emory, and all my people about Asher taking over Saul's business.

Apparently, Asher went behind Saul's back, jacked up Saul's credit to the limit, and used the money to buy out all of Saul's imported inventory. Dante and I don't have a business deal without that inventory.

Asher would have gotten away with destroying both Dante and me if this went through.

There's just one teeny, weeny little problem. Saul's credit isn't good enough to sustain all that debt. Saul's credit is imploding, which means all that inventory will revert back to the supplier unless someone pays for it upfront.

Dante is launching a massive fraud lawsuit against Asher. Dante wants me to be one of the co-plaintiffs on the suit. I tell him to send over the paperwork so I can sign everything. We're going to take this one all the way to the top if we have to.

I don't tell Melody any of that. She doesn't need to hear that when she doesn't even know if her father will live or die.

I don't remind her of all the things Saul did wrong. I don't remind her that she never would have been in danger from Asher if not for Saul's mistakes.

None of that matters right now. I don't need to talk about Saul, not even to say anything good or bad about him. None of this has anything to do with me.

What Saul did or didn't do is between him and Melody. My only job is to be here for her.

I'm her husband. She's my wife. Where else would I be?

She wanted something real and now we have it. I don't even know the moment when it happened. I don't know when we stopped being casual hookup buddies and became....this.

Yes, I do. I know the exact moment when it happened. It happened when I found out some asshole kidnapped her, threatened her, and took her from me.

She's mine. I know that now. I'll never let anyone come near her again, especially not some murderous psycho who would threaten his own sister....for a business deal. No way in hell.

I put my juice down on the chair next to me. We have the waiting room to ourselves, which is just as well. I don't want anyone disturbing Melody.

She has no family left. Saul and Asher are her only family. Now Asher is gone. He'll never be her family again regardless of what happens to him legally.

I don't know what will happen to Saul, but I have to be that for Melody now. I have to be the one who holds her up and protects her.

I have to be her foundation so she doesn't drift off into the vast reaches of space. She might not come back if she did that.

My phone buzzes in my pocket again. My phone has been buzzing non-stop since we got here.

I stretch out my leg to take out my phone when four doctors come in from the operating room. All of them are still wearing their scrubs, caps, and their face masks hang around their necks. They must have just finished with Saul.

Melody and I stand up and walk over there to meet them. "Well?" she pants. "How is he?"

"I'm afraid the damage to his internal organs is irreversible," an older male doctor replies. "The fall shattered his pelvis, broke his spine, and ruptured multiple organs. We've stabilized him as much as we can, but I'm afraid it's only a matter of time at this point. You can go in and see him, but you won't have much time. I'm sorry, but there's nothing more we can do to prolong his life. He's barely hanging on as it is."

She howls in despair and her hand flies to her mouth. I move in and pull her into my arms, but she barely notices.

The doctors give me a pained look over her head and leave us alone.

She wails in my ear while I hold her tight. So that's it. Saul will die. It's only a matter of time.

"Asher killed him!" she screams. "Asher killed my father!"

I kiss the side of her head and straighten her up. She still stands there covering her mouth, but she can't hold back her sobs.

"Come on, baby," I tell her. "You have to go see him. You have to spend as much time with him as you can. You don't want to miss a single moment. Come on. Let's go."

I take her hand and lead her into the back. She won't stop crying all the way there.

I have to handle this. I have to make sure she doesn't fall apart so much that she misses her father's last moments.

He already apologized to her at the estate. He probably wants to do it again and to tell her how much he loves her.

She needs that. She needs these last few moments with her father. She can cry for a year after he's gone. She can't miss this.

I check with the nurses at the desk and find out where Saul is. They're already expecting us.

I lead her to Saul's room. He lies on his back with an IV going into his arm. He doesn't have any masks or tubes going into his mouth or face.

He doesn't look like he's dying. He just looks weak and tired.

He smiles when I lead Melody sobbing her guts out. She stumbles over to the bed and grabs his hand. "Daddy......" she moans.

He still has enough strength to squeeze her hand. "My beautiful baby....." His voice comes out as a barely audible breath. "I love you. I'm proud of you. Everything is going to be all right."

"Don't die, Daddy....!" she bawls. "I need you!"

"You're stronger than you know....." His eyes dart in my direction. "You won't be alone. You're going to be all right."

"Don't leave me, Daddy!" she chokes. "Don't leave me alone."

"You aren't alone. Niko will take care of you. He'll show you what to do. Everything is going to work out for you. I know it."

She breaks down in wordless sobs. I have to walk up behind her and put my arm around her. I can't let her go through this alone.

He raises his hand, clasps her cheek, and raises his head to look her dead in the eyes. "Listen to me, sweetheart. You're everything good about this family. You're my prize and my jewel. Don't do what I did. Make it good. Make everything good. You can do it. You're the only one who can. I know you can. I'm proud of you. Always remember that in the future. Whatever you do, I know you'll make me proud."

"What....what do you mean? Make what good?"

He sinks back on his pillows and gazes on her with a beautiful, beaming smile of pure love.

"I love you," he whispers. "I believe in you. You'll make everything good again. I know you will."

His eyes drift shut and his hand and arm sink back down onto the mattress at his side.

She attacks him, grabs his hand, and tries to shake him. "Daddy!" she shrieks. "Daddy—no!!"

I take hold of her shoulders and try to pull her away.

"DADDY!!" she screeches. "DADDY—DON'T YOU DARE LEAVE ME!!"

He doesn't respond. The heart rate machine at his bedside goes into a steady beep that doesn't end. One of the nurses comes in and shuts it off.

Melody doesn't see or hear any of that. She shakes her father harder. "DADDY!!" she screams. "DADDY!!"

I can't keep letting her go through this. I grip her shoulders tighter and physically pull her away from him.

She keeps trying to fight me, throws her elbow at me, and dives for him when I dodge out of the way.

She starts shaking and calling for him again. I can't let this go on.

I move in front of her, use my body to block her from going near him, take hold of her shoulders, and steer her out of the room by main force.

She keeps struggling all the way out to the waiting room. She doesn't stop until I park her in the same spot outside the doors. It's over. He's gone.

She looks around everywhere in frantic anxiety like she might try to fight me to get back in there. I plant myself in front of her. She isn't going anywhere.

She takes one look into my eyes and breaks down sobbing again. At least she can let it out now.

I fold her in my arms. Relief floods me that she can cry now. Saul is gone. He was the last of her family. I'm all she has left.

Asher is as good as dead to her. She needs all the help she can get—from me and anyone else who cares about her.

I hold her for a long time, but she doesn't stop crying. She might not stop—not for days, weeks, or even months.

I don't want her hanging around here—not right outside the ward where her father just died.

I put my arm behind her waist and steer her out of the hospital. We both need to get the hell out of here.

I put her in the limo and tell the driver to take us to my penthouse. We'll never go back to the honeymoon suite. That time is over.

Melody is either with me or she isn't. She's my wife. She's going home with me if she's going anywhere.

We aren't on our honeymoon anymore. We might not be going to have a real marriage that goes the distance. We might both decide to end this experiment tomorrow.

Whatever happens won't happen in the honeymoon suite. We're living in the real world now.

She cries all the way home and all the way up the elevator. She cries all the way to my bedroom.

I pull down the covers and tuck her into my bed. I sit down on the mattress outside the covers and rub her back, stroke her hair, and give her occasional kisses on the side of the head while she cries. She can stay here as long as she needs to.

I send my concierge a text to tell him to bring all our stuff back here from the hotel. I also tell him to buy a new set of pajamas in the same style but with a different color pattern than her old ones.

I don't want her remembering her time with Asher—not unless she has to. She'll have a hard enough time putting all of this behind her.

I give her one last kiss and leave her there to go out to the kitchen. It's getting toward dinnertime, but I don't feel like making anything too fancy.

I don't suppose she wants to eat much anyway, so I keep it simple and make her another sandwich. She can probably handle that. I cut up a piece of fruit and stick it on the side of the plate.

I make another plate for myself, take both back to the bedroom, and sit down on the other side of the bed with my back propped against the headboard.

"Come here, baby," I tell her. "Eat something and let's watch a movie together."

She crawls into my arms still sniffing and wiping her nose on her shirt cuff. It's already a mess.

I hand her a box of tissues, grab the remote, turn on the TV, and start flipping through the streaming menu.

"Life of Brian, Animal House, or *Caddyshack?"* I ask.

"Caddyshack," she croaks.

I chuckle to myself. "You are such a sucker."

She giggles and pulls her plate toward her. She props it on my lap next to mine so she can eat and cuddle with me at the same time.

I start the movie, kiss her hair, and take a bite of my sandwich. I run my fingers through her hair and rub her back while we both eat.

I can live with this and so can she. This movie will end. Then hopefully she'll be able to get some sleep before we both have to deal with big, bad reality again.

Chapter 27: Niko

I wait for the chauffeur to open the door for me to get out of the limo. I instinctively glance around for any sign of danger before I extend my hand into the limo to help Melody get out.

She straightens up wearing a sleek navy blue business suit, sky-high pumps, and a gold pin in her ruffled blouse collar.

She locks her eyes on me. "How do I look? Do I look professional enough?"

"You look great—and no one expects you to be professional. You're the bereaved here. No one expects you to function."

She glances toward the office building behind us. "I'm sure glad you're here. I couldn't do this by myself."

I take her hand and squeeze. "That's what I'm here for. Just remember what I said. If you get in over your head, just signal me with a glance or something and I'll step in. Understand? You don't have to handle everything."

She nods. "Thank you. I'm really grateful."

"Stop it." I take a chance and give her a peck on the lips. "You're my wife, remember? What else would I be doing?"

She doesn't blush or even smile. Her eyes keep darting to the building behind us. She's too petrified to think straight.

I turn away and lead her by the hand to the front steps leading to the building entrance. She hangs back. I have to keep going to pull her into the building.

She keeps remembering to follow me before she hesitates again. I don't blame her.

I feel her shaking when we get into the elevator and ride up to the eleventh floor. I check in with the receptionist. "Miss Melody Gottlieb is here to see Salvatore Rossi."

"Yes, Sir," the receptionist replies. "You can go right in—fourth door on the left. Everyone is waiting for you."

Melody stumbles again when we walk down the hallway to the conference room. I have to tow her into a room full of ten men in business suits. They all sit on one side of the enormous table.

I approach them from the other side and shake hands with everyone. I keep a hold on Melody's hand, but she seems to come back to her senses once we get into the room.

She smiles, shakes hands with everyone, and tells them all that it's a pleasure to meet them.

The two of us sit down alone on this side of the table. We sit in front of Salvatore, Saul's lawyer. Salvatore opens his laptop, folds his hands on top of the table, and leans toward us.

"As you know, Miss Gottlieb, your father left his entire fortune and all his assets to you and your brother."

Melody lowers her eyes to the tabletop. "I thought so."

Salvatore consults his computer. "We've consulted with the Police Department and the District Attorney about the case against your brother. He's pleading guilty to the fraud, embezzlement, kidnapping, and attempted murder charges. He's also declining to fight the fraud lawsuit being brought by Mr. Helme and Mr. Holloway. Mr. Helme consulted with our team last week—prior to your father's death. Mr.

Helme offered to let your father join him and Mr. Holloway as a co-plaintiff in the fraud lawsuit against your brother. We advised that we would encourage your father to participate in this suit. We're also the executors of his estate until it gets handed over to his heirs—which means it's now up to us if his estate participates in the suit."

Melody blinks at him in confused shock. How much of this is actually penetrating her brain? "What does that mean?" she asks.

"Your brother isn't fighting either the criminal charges or the lawsuit. It means that your brother is automatically liable for compensatory damages to all the injured parties. All the money, assets, and inventory he defrauded from your father will return to the parties from which he stole them. He stole them from your father—which means they all return to the estate. Since he is no longer a qualified heir to your father's assets, that leaves you."

Her eyes fall out of their sockets. "Are you saying.....are you saying I'm my father's sole heir?"

"Yes, Ma'am. That's exactly what I'm saying." Salvatore turns back to his computer. "In addition to the ongoing enterprise with Mr. Holloway and Mr. Helme, your father had fourteen active corporations operating under five different parent companies. You'll need to arrange to meet with their governing and executive boards to orchestrate the handover. We'll arrange a time for you to come in and sign over all your father's bank accounts, real estate assets, chattels, confidential files, and the like."

Melody stares at him in a daze. Now I know nothing more is going to get through her head. I squeeze her hand under the table and she jumps practically out of her skin.

It's time for me to do my thing. I stand up and extend my hand across the table. "Thank you for all your diligence, Mr. Rossi. I think Miss Gottlieb needs to go home and process all of this before she makes any life-changing business decisions. You can email her or me about how you would like her to proceed—but I don't think she'll be ready to do anything until after the funeral."

"Of course not." He shakes my hand. "It will take time for us to process all the paperwork with the Police Department, District Attorney's office, and Mr. Gottlieb Jr.'s defense counsel. We'll be in touch as soon as we're ready to move forward."

I thank everyone present even though I don't even know who half of them are. Melody barely notices when I lead her outside and put her back in the limo.

She doesn't seem to be aware of me. I don't want to take her home like this, so I tell the chauffeur to drop us off at Central Park.

I take her hand and lead her around the lawns, parks, fountains, statues, and streams for a while.

Families with kids play and laugh all around us. It's a normal day for all of them. They don't know a seismic shift in the business world just happened a few blocks away.

I stop at Gapstow Bridge and stare off into the trees. I'm not sure what else I can do for Melody—apart from just be here for her.

This inheritance changes things for me, too. She isn't Saul's sheltered daughter anymore.

This inheritance puts her in the same category with all the other members of The Billionaires' Club. She's a billionaire, just like that.

Does she even realize what this means? Her life is going to change after this and not because she lost her only two living relatives in the space of a few hours.

Her scratchy voice brings me out of my thoughts. "I can't believe it!" she husks.

I glance over at her. She stares over the side of the bridge into the trees, too.

"I guess it makes sense," I tell her. "It isn't like they were going to hand your father's assets to Asher after what he did. That leaves you."

"What am I supposed to do with it all?" she chokes. "I don't know how to run a multi-million-dollar corporation! I don't know anything about business! My father never taught me."

"It's simple. You either learn how to run them yourself or you get someone else to do it for you."

Her head snaps around. "You could do it! You know all about this stuff. You're great at business."

I raise both hands and shake my head. "No, no! It can't be me! I'm too close to the situation—and you and I are involved with each other even if we don't stay together. I have a conflict of interest. It would breed resentment between us. You wouldn't be able to trust that I wasn't skewing the whole thing in my favor."

"Well, how am I supposed to trust anyone else?" Her hand flies to her head. "Holy crap! We're talking about billions of dollars in assets and operating budgets!"

I nod. "Yeah. Your father had a big empire. I guess he still does."

"Then how am I supposed to choose someone to run all of that on my behalf? How do I know who's trustworthy and who is out to screw me over? How would I be able to trust anyone and not start suspecting them of skewing it in their own favor?"

I can only shrug. "That's the problem every businessperson faces. That's the temptation to do everything yourself. You can't do everything yourself even if you're heavily involved from the top. You just have to keep an eye on things and choose wisely when you hire someone."

"If I'm going to keep an eye on things and choose wisely when I hire someone, then I might as well be heavily involved from the top. I would be heavily involved from the top either way. I would have to be. I wouldn't be able to sleep at night if I didn't run things myself."

"Yeah. That's it in a nutshell. We're all in the same boat. I certainly a m."

She blinks at me. "I can't believe this! I'm....I'm....I have to become like you."

I find myself gazing into her eyes. "Don't you see what this means?"

Her brow furrows. "What do you mean?"

"Your father's last words. He must have realized when he was dying that his fortune would go to you. All this time, he planned for Asher to take over for him. He must have realized on his deathbed that Asher would lose everything and all your father's assets would go to you. This is what he meant by making it good and doing it in a way he couldn't. He meant for you to take over his business and run it the right way."

She covers her face and groans. "Oh, my God! I can't believe this is happening!"

I put my arm around her shoulders. "You're going to be great. You're a decent person. I'm sure his business will only benefit from having a person with scruples and integrity running it instead of trying to manipulate the situation into some kind of Frankenstein monster. The deal between you, me, and Dante will only thrive, now that you're involved."

Her head shoots up and her eyes spark with fire. "I'm in the deal?!"

"Of course. You're taking over your father's share of it."

"You mean.....I have to handle.....imports....and inventories.....and purchase agreements....."

"Yeah. That's what he did."

She looks away as her eyes slip out of focus. It's a lot to take in. Her mind churns in a million directions.

I don't break in on her thoughts. She has a steep learning curve in front of her, but I believe in her. She's going to become something so much greater than she was.

I take her hand and lead her away into the park. I don't want her to think about any of that right now, but I already know she has to. She's going to be thinking about nothing else for a long time.

Chapter 28: Niko

I lead Melody back to Strawberry Fields. We stand around, lean against the stone walls, and watch children playing.

Some guys play Ultimate Frisbee on the lawn. A few dogs run around barking excitedly. They try to get involved in the frisbee game and make the guys laugh at them.

I have to break the silence again. "I'm prepared to dissolve the marriage before you sign off on your father's assets. I know you don't want to share your wealth with me....."

She spins around fast. "Yes, I do!"

"You do?" Now it's my turn to frown. "Are you sure?"

"Yes, Niko! Don't you dare talk about dissolving the marriage! I want us to stay together—especially now! I need you to help me with this! Who else am I supposed to learn from? You're the only person in my life that I'm certain has my best interest at heart."

"But......are you sure you won't resent me for that? I mean....I don't want to step in and start doing it all for you....."

"I don't mean that you would do it all for me. I'll do it. I'll run my father's empire. You're right that it would come between us if you did it. I only mean I need you to help me learn. I don't understand this stuff. You do. I need you."

I study her. She really said those words. I have to gulp before I say, "I need you, too. I don't want to lose you."

She rushes me, throws her arms around my neck, and clings to me. "I can't ever lose you again! Don't ever talk about dissolving the marriage."

I slip my arms around her waist and close my eyes in her hair. I can finally let go in the certainty that she's mine. I've never needed anyone as much as this.

"I couldn't stand it when Asher took you away from me," I breathe. "No one will ever take you away from me again. I swear it."

She squeezes me tighter. Damn, she feels good!

She lets go, smiles up at me for the first time, and takes my hand. "Let's go home."

We set off for the park. Helping her handle her father's business is going to be a learning curve for me, but not as much as being married to her.

We're doing this. We're going to build a real marriage and a real future. This is all going to be real. I don't know if I can handle all of that, but I have to. I have to do it for her and for me.

I call the limo back and we go home to the penthouse. That's home for both of us now. She'll never leave.

She goes into the bedroom to change out of her suit. I'm just passing the door when I hear her phone chime. She stares at the screen and groans.

"What's wrong, baby?" I ask. "Don't tell me it's more bad news."

"It's an email from Salvatore with the list of my father's assets." She throws her phone on the bed. "I can't look at this right now. I need junk food."

I stop in front of her and study her from above. Then I slip my hand into my pocket.

My fingers close around a velvet ring box. I've been carrying this box around in my pocket for three days while I try to decide when, where, and how to propose to her.

I'm already married to her, but I never got a chance to propose to her—not the right way.

I might not get another chance, so I drop on one knee in front of her, open the box in front of her, and hold it out for her to see. "Melody Gottlieb, will you please do me the honor of being my wife for the rest of my life—for better or for worse, for richer or for poorer, in sickness and in health, and all that other stuff?"

She stares at the ring. It's a beautiful princess-cut diamond engagement ring. She's already wearing her engagement ring and wedding band, but I didn't buy her those rings.

Dante and her father used investment funds from the business deal to buy the rings out of our promotion budget. That's all our engagement and wedding were—a business promotion.

I don't want her wearing those rings anymore. I want to sell them and put the money back into the deal.

Her eyes shoot up to mine and melt in two puddles of tears. Her face screws up in a mess of spasms. "Yes!" she chokes. "Yes, I'll marry you!"

I find myself laughing and my hands shake when I pull the ring out of the box. I take off her old engagement ring, slip on the new one, and stash the old one in the box in my pocket. Neither of us ever has to look at it again.

She waits just long enough for me to put the box away before she lunges off the bed, tackles me with her arms around my neck, and topples me onto the floor.

She kisses me a thousand times. "I love you, Niko! I'm going to be the best wife in the world to you."

I laugh again. "You already are the best wife in the world to me, baby. You don't have to do anything but be your perfect, beautiful self."

She dives for me and starts kissing me, but that kiss softens in a minute. Her body vibrates with sexual tension and desire, but she slows herself down to make it more fluid and romantic.

I stroke her sides and squeeze her ass, but I don't take it any further. I don't want my proposal to turn into that.

I'll have all the time in the world to own her body and conquer her in new ways neither of us ever dreamed of.

She undulates her breasts down on top of me and then spreads her knees to straddle me. She keeps rocking her hips in luscious beats against me. She's getting more turned on by the second.

I love feeling how much she wants me. I love feeling that she wants to give herself to me.

She strokes her hand down my cheeks and plays with my hair while we kiss. We both keep our eyes open.

I don't want to take her when I look into her eyes. I mean, I always want to take her, but looking at her like this means something so much more.

She's going to become one of the richest women in the country. She's going to become a high-powered business CEO just like all my friends in The Billionaires' Club. She might even become a member in her own right.

I admire her so much more now than I did before—and not because she inherited all this money.

I admire the fact that she's willing to take the bull by the horns and learn how to do it right.

She takes her father's words seriously. She'll make it good. She'll avoid the pitfalls that destroyed him. She'll become something so much better than he was. She already is something so much better than he was.

I love her for that. I love everything about her on the inside. Her body is just the bonus that makes it all so much better.

She must realize that I don't plan to take her like this—not after I just proposed to her. She sits up, rides me for another minute, and then climbs off.

She sits down on the floor and looks around the room without seeing anything. "What am I supposed to do first?"

"Why don't you read Salvatore's email? Read the documentation he sent over."

She makes a face at me. "That isn't what I want to hear."

I laugh at her. "Get ready to hear a lot of things you don't want to hear. You're going to become everyone's go-to girl whenever they can't solve a problem on their own. They're going to land in your office expecting you to handle it, so get used to it."

I sit up, stand up, and give her my hand to pull her to her feet.

"Come on," I tell her. "Bring your phone to the living room, bite the bullet, and read the documentation. Then I'll be able to answer any questions you have before you hear from him again."

"Fine," she grumbles. "Be reasonable like that."

I laugh and head out to the living room. She grabs her phone and follows me.

I pull open the fridge to find something to make for lunch. She opens her phone and leans her hip against the counter while she scrolls.

"Holy Mother of Jesus!" she chokes. "These bank account balances are astronomical."

I look over her shoulder while I put a dish of potatoes au gratin in front of her. "That's normal for that size company. Just remember that includes payroll, operating costs, legal, marketing, HR—everything."

"Still! I didn't think it was this big. Oh, my God!" She gasps and her hand flies to her head.

"What's wrong?" I try to see over her shoulder while I stick a fork in her hand.

"My father is listed as the CEO of each of the five parent companies."

"Yeah? So? That isn't unusual."

"He's drawing a salary from all of them! Each of the salaries is over ten million dollars."

I nod. "That sounds about right."

"It sounds about right?!" she shrieks. "Are you crazy?! That means *I'm* going to start drawing all those salaries!"

"That's right. So you better learn how to do the job so you earn it."

"Are you nuts?!" she roars. "I can't start earning that kind of money! I would bankrupt the company—or companies—all of them!"

"Not likely. Your father has been drawing these salaries for years. He didn't bankrupt the company."

"But you said he used shady business practices! You said he would tank the deal by being worse off than he pretended to be!" I cover my eyes. "I can't draw these salaries! This is out of the question!"

I take her hand down. "Listen to me, baby. Your father's shady business practices didn't have anything to do with drawing these salaries. Every big-time CEO is drawing salaries like this. I am."

Her jaw drops. "You are?"

"Of course. I earn it by being the last stop for anything that goes wrong in the entire company. I'm the one carrying all that responsibility on my shoulders."

"Yeah, but.....that's you."

"It isn't just me. Every man in The Billionaires' Club is doing the same thing. Dante is doing it. They're all doing it. It's normal."

She frowns. "It is?"

"Yes. Your father overleveraged his debt and spent money on things he didn't need. He got himself into deals he couldn't afford or the numbers were off. He tried to outmaneuver people to take more than his rightful share of the profits. That's what he did wrong. It had nothing to do with him drawing a CEO's salary from multiple parent companies."

She blinks down at her phone. "Oh. I didn't know."

"What else did Salvatore send over?"

She bends over the counter reading on her phone. "He included the latest shareholder prospectuses from all the companies my father owns stock in—which is every company in his whole portfolio. It's going to take me some time to read all of that." She scrolls some more. "Here are the names and contact details of all the governing and executive board members I'm supposed to meet with to arrange the handover....."

I sidle up behind her while she reads. She doesn't notice me until I bend over her, grab her hips, and use my weight to drive her body into the counter.

She gasps once, tries to correct so she can keep reading, and fails.

Her voice quavers when she tries to turn around. "Niko....."

"Do you feel that, baby?" I drive my hardness into her ass. "Do you feel how hot you make me?"

She gasps again and moans. She shoots me on wild glance over her shoulder and makes a split second of eye contact with me before she looks away.

I slide my hands around her hips and rake my fingernails up her thighs. She makes me so damn hard when she bends over like that. She doesn't even know she's sticking her ass out to tempt me.

I bite her shoulder through her shirt. Her body erupts under me.

She can't get away when I drive into her. She makes me so insanely hot that I have to take her right now.

I tug up her skirt and she whines when she grinds her hips back into me. Her ass crushes my hard prick and a bomb goes off in my mind.

This is my woman—my wife. I'm going to enjoy her in so many ways, starting right here on the kitchen counter.

She's already bending over and shoving her ass out to meet me, but I push her down harder anyway. I lean all the way over her and growl in her ear while I pull her skirt the rest of the way up.

I'm exploding for her. I have to take her right now.

I rip her panties aside and nothing can hold back the primal insanity as I drive all the way in. She screams once and then doesn't stop as I hammer in as hard as I can.

I slam her against the counter, but she's already falling apart in my hands. She throws back her head and arches her hips to take my thrusts. I can't even form words for how hot she is.

I feel myself losing control, but she matches me all the way. As hard as I thrust into her, she encourages me by winding her hips back into every cruel penetration.

I gasp for breath through gritted teeth. She sobs and moans in between screams of torrential passion. Holy shit, I can't take this!

She flattens her chest against the counter and presses her head back into mine as we both spiral out into space. I explode inside her, but her channel is already spasming around me in wicked little clenching convulsions.

Her wetness gushes over me as the cataclysm hits me. I fall all the way on top of her still pumping my heart and soul into her.

She keeps thrashing under me with every stroke. I can't get enough of her. I already feel myself getting hard for another round. Tonight is going to be a long night and I'm just getting started.

That's okay because we're married. I don't have to go anywhere or do anything. She's mine.

She'll be mine forever—mine to enjoy, mine to cherish, mine to protect. Nothing can ever break that now.

Chapter 29:
Melody

I startle out of a sound sleep and jolt upright in bed when I feel someone try to grab me. It takes me a second before I recognize Niko's smell.

He's moving around in bed. We're in his bedroom in his penthouse—except that this is our bedroom in our penthouse now. We're married. We're married for real.

This room is much darker than the bedroom at the Mandarin Oriental or the bedroom at Shadow Glen Estates. I can't see anything.

I feel him stroke my back. "It's all right," he murmurs. "It's just me. I have to go to the bathroom. I'm not going anywhere."

I collapse back on the cushions while he slips out of bed. I hear his footsteps cross the bedroom and go into the bathroom.

He shuts the door before he turns the light on. Barely a crack of light shines around the door. I want to drift off again.....and I do.

I drift off until he comes back in the dark, sits down on the mattress, and slides between the sheets next to me.

He wraps his arms around me and sinks down. We're both too exhausted from all this sex to do anything other than sleep.

I hug him tight. He's mine and I'm his. I don't want or need anything else.

I'm just about to fade out again when I hear a cell phone ring in the distance. I try to ignore it. Niko stiffens. "Now what?" he mutters.

"Just leave it alone," I mumble. "You can answer it in the morning."

"No one should be calling me at this time of night. It might be something important."

He drags himself out of bed again. I still can't see anything until he switches on the bedside lamp.

He rummages around the room until he finds his pants on the floor. He pulls out the phone, frowns at the screen, and then answers the call. "Hello? Yes, this is Niko Holloway."

He listens for a long time and his expression turns to solid ice. I don't like where this is going.

He finally says, "Yeah, I got it. Thank you for calling. I'll handle it. Bye."

He hangs up and sits down on the edge of the bed facing away from me. He doesn't stop frowning at his phone.

"What's going on?" I ask.

"Asher just got out on bail. I'm calling in my security team."

I freeze on my pillow. "He's...out on bail? How can he be? He pled guilty to kidnapping and attempted murder."

"It's worse than that. He's facing an additional murder charge for your father's death and he's planning to plead guilty to that, too. His defense attorney got Asher four weeks to get his affairs in order before he turns himself in to serve his sentence."

I shoot out of bed. "What?! That's ridiculous! He's dangerous!"

"I know, baby," Niko murmurs over his shoulder. "We can't reverse the judge's decision. We can only take the necessary precautions to make sure he doesn't do anything."

He holds the phone to his ear. Then he stands up, goes around the room, and starts using one hand to pull on his pants.

He gets on the line with someone or other and starts ordering all kinds of security for the penthouse, the building, his offices, business, premises, and drivers.

I can't lie here listening to this. I get out of bed, put on my pajamas, and then my bathrobe.

It's two o'clock in the morning, but it looks like we aren't going to get any more sleep tonight.

I go to the kitchen and put on a pot of coffee. Maybe all of this will come to nothing. Maybe Asher really will put his affairs in order and go off to prison where he belongs without bothering anyone else.

I know better than to believe that. He's out of his mind. He threatened to kill me once. He probably got himself released on bail just so he could come back and finish the job.

He'll probably hold it against me for the rest of his life that I inherited my father's fortune. Asher has been planning to take over my father's empire for years.

Now the dream is over and he's going to prison for murdering his own father. That has to hurt.

I'm just pouring coffee into two cups and adding milk and sugar to Niko's when he comes in with the phone still glued to his ear. He's still wearing his pants and nothing else.

He talks in between listening. He moves the phone away from his mouth to kiss me and say, "Thank you," before he picks up his mug and walks away.

He paces around the penthouse, looks through the blinds, and gives descriptions of the surrounding buildings and streets.

He finally downs the rest of his coffee, hangs up, and comes back to the kitchen.

He grabs the coffee pot and pours himself a second cup. "The security team is on its way over right now, baby. I want you to promise me you won't leave the apartment without them protecting you."

I smile at him. "I promise. I don't want to meet Asher in the wrong place at the wrong time."

"It's only for a month. Then he'll be behind bars and we can go back to what we were doing."

"Who called you to tell you that Asher got out?" I ask.

"It was the DA. He argued his hardest to keep Asher off the streets, but Asher hasn't been convicted of murder yet. He already pled guilty to the other charges, but the judge can only sentence him for the charges he's already pled guilty to—which means he would be entitled to a grace period before he turns himself in." Niko raises both hands. "I don't make the rules. The guy should have been sent to the gas chamber by now if I had my way."

I wince. "I probably wouldn't go that far."

"I would. He kidnapped you and would have killed you if I hadn't intervened. He killed your father. He's a cold-blooded murderer. He sure as hell doesn't belong walking around free on the streets."

Another phone call interrupts him. He answers it. "Yeah. Okay. Come on up." He hangs up and taps his phone. "The security team is on their way up. They're going to come inside the apartment and take a look around before they decide if they need to station some guys i nside."

"Just promise me they won't be in our bedroom."

He smirks. "No, they won't be. I don't want them seeing anything."

I turn bright red, but right then, someone knocks on the door.

"That's them." He goes over to answer it. He pulls the door open and a gunshot blasts from out in the hall.

Niko staggers back once before Asher storms in and shoots Niko straight in the chest a second time.

"NIKO!!" I shriek, but it's too late. Niko topples onto the carpet covered in blood.

Asher wheels in my direction and stalks toward me aiming his gun at me. This isn't my brother. Niko is right. Asher is a cold-blooded murderer.

He must have been waiting for the security team to show up so he could break into the penthouse first.

He brings a high-powered rifle this time, jams his gun into his shoulder, and his fingers tighten around the trigger grip. I relive the moment when he aimed his handgun at me at the estate. He's going to kill me. He's a psycho and he's going to kill me.

I stand frozen to the spot. I'm trapped in the apartment with a raving gunman. I can't get out.

Asher shot Niko. Is Niko dying over there on the floor?

I glance in his direction, but Niko isn't there anymore. My brain takes a second to switch gears before he rockets out of nowhere. He comes from behind Asher and knocks Asher out of the way just as the gun goes off.

Niko collides with me and tackles me to the ground. His blood soaks through my pajamas, but Asher is already scrambling to get to his feet.

Niko rolls over and then flips all the way onto his back on top of me.

Asher stands up and curls his lips back from his teeth when he levels the gun at both of us.

Niko flattens himself on top of me. His bloody back lies squashed on top of my chest and stomach. He spreads his arms to protect me with his body. Asher can't shoot me without killing Niko in the process—if Asher hasn't killed Niko already.

I want to push Niko off me. I want to put my own body in front of Niko's to protect *him* from Asher. I can't let Asher shoot Niko a third time. It might already be too late. I can't live with that.

Niko's breath strains. He pants for air and his breathing gets shorter and shallower. He starts to relax into me.

I want to yell out for him, but at that moment, a bunch of burly gunmen in black business suits invade the apartment through the open door.

They're all armed. They take one look at Asher as he spins around to point his gun at them.

They open fire and he jerks a dozen times before he collapses on the floor.

"NIKO!!" I shriek and clamber out from under him.

He groans when he flops on the floor. I paw at his pants pocket and grab his phone to call 911.

The security guys swarm the apartment and then pull me away from Niko so they can start doing first aid on him.

I can't look at him. I have to turn away so I can concentrate on giving my report to the emergency operator. She tells me the Police and ambulance are on the way here right now.

Chapter 30: Melody

I sit in a chair next to Niko's bed and stare at the side of his face. A tube goes into his mouth. It keeps inflating his chest to breathe for him before it lets him exhale.

I don't want to stop staring at him. He saved my life again. He protected me with his body when he'd already been shot twice.

God, I love him so much! He's a hero.

He wouldn't want me to waste this time just admiring him, so I pick up my phone and go back to reading the documentation about my father's many businesses. They're my businesses now.

The information makes more sense the longer I read it. I have to search up some terms and concepts on the internet, but I'm learning. I'm getting the hang of this.

Having Niko here to explain it to me would be better, but he'll recover from this. The doctors say he'll be going home as soon as he gets the all-clear from his surgery.

The bullets hit his lungs, but the doctors repaired all the damage. His heart and major blood vessels are all fine.

Niko will get his strength back. Then he and I will go on as before. I'll love him back from this. He's too strong to let something like this keep him down.

I'm just telling myself not to keep looking at him when someone walks into the hospital room behind me.

Dante Helme stops next to my chair, stares at Niko for a minute, and then winces when he looks down at me. "How is he?" Dante husks.

"He's gonna be okay. The doctors say he's going to make a complete recovery."

Dante wilts in relief. "Phew! I was so worried when I got your call!" He frowns at me. "Are you okay?"

I try to smile at him. "I'm okay. I wasn't at first, but I am now. He'll be all right. He'll recover from this."

"Did the Police give you a hard time about it? You let me know if you need any legal help."

Now I really do smile at him. "Thank you, but they didn't give me any trouble. The security guys were all witnesses that Asher was holding us at gunpoint when they rushed in. It isn't like Niko or I ever threatened Asher."

"I guess so." Dante frowns at me. "Listen....you probably don't want to hear this from me.....but....you know......you're a billionaire now."

I turn bright red and look away. "Don't remind me."

"Hey! I meant you could join the club. We would all love to have you....and we could give you information—and advice if you want it. I know you're gonna have your own certified expert at home and everything, but if you want help with anything, we're all here for you. You should come to one of our meetings sometime. I can introduce you to everyone. You don't have to do this alone. That's what we're here for."

I smile at him and wind up blushing. "I really appreciate that. I do. I'm grateful. I need all the help I can get."

He bursts into a grin. "Hey! We're business partners now, remember?"

"Yeah. We are." I beam at him. "I hope I can be the kind of business partner you deserve. I hope I can correct some of the mistakes my father made. I want you to know I don't plan to continue the way he did. I'm gonna do it right."

"I'm sure you will. I know you aren't like him. I won't say I'm glad he's dead, but I am glad that you're my business partner now. You and Niko....you're perfect for each other."

I lower my eyes. "Thank you. I hope so."

"I know so." He points at my phone. "I'm only a phone call away if you need me for anything."

"Thank you. I will probably take you up on that."

He squeezes my shoulder. "I won't keep you. I'll email you later.... and I'll have Kevin Drake contact you about applying to join the club. You would be an asset to us. I'll see you around sometime."

He slips out of the room and leaves me alone.

I go back to gazing at Niko. We're on the same level now. I'm a billionaire married to another billionaire.

I'm going to join The Billionaires' Club. I never thought I'd see the interior of that place.

I can't wait to get started. I don't have to rely on Niko for support and information.

Dante is right. I'll be living under the same roof with a bona fide expert, but it sure is nice to know that I have all these other amazing people to call on, too.

I'm not as alone as I thought I was. This new chapter of my life is opening up my world in ways it never opened up before. I can't wait to get out there and conquer it. This is going to be great.

End of Book 3.

Keep Reading

The Billionaires' Club Series: Book 4: Rising Star

Derek Salazar used to be one of the richest, most powerful, influential members of The Billionaires' Club. Then he lost everything when Apico Acquisitions carried out a hostile takeover of Derek's company.

Now he's working as a penniless salesman in the deepest, darkest, most forgotten corner of New Jersey. He's a nobody and everyone treats him as one—everyone except his employer's admin clerk.

Vivian Cooper doesn't see anything special about Derek—except that he's the only person in the office who treats her like a real person. Could this be the beginning of something extraordinary—or the path to ultimate heartbreak and destruction for both of them?

You can find it at your favorite book retailer.

Get All of AE Moran's Free Books

S ign Up Once—Get all A.E. Moran's free books including brand new releases

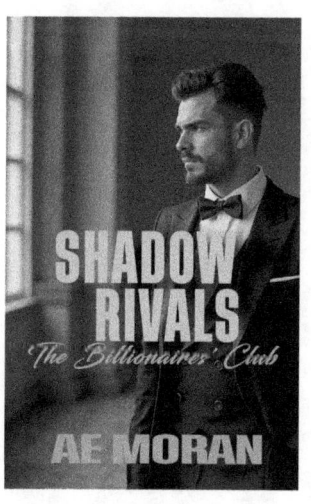

Holden Seager is hot, magnetic, and filthy, stinking, obscenely rich. He commands a room the minute he walks in the door. So what happens when meets another shark as powerful, as charismatic, and as successful as he is—not to mention ten years younger? When these two meet across the negotiating table, one of them will walk away the undisputed winner. The other will walk away with nothing.

Or so it seems.

Unless they're best friends.

When the business deal of a lifetime falls flat on its face and neither of these titans knows how to bring it back to life, this might be the opportunity Dayna Turner has been waiting for.

There's just one problem. She works as an assistant to one of these powerful men....and she's in love with the other. It's a recipe for disaster and heartbreak—unless Dayna can pull off an even bigger coup that will leave them all richer, happier, and more closely connected than ever. The alternative is the destruction of everything all three of them have worked so hard to build.

Sign up at www.authoraemoran.com to read it for free.

About AE Moran

A.E Moran is the contemporary romance pen name for Theo Mann.

I write 70 books per year—and yes, before you ask, all these books are my original creative work. Nothing written under my name is AI-generated or ghostwritten because I write better than AI and any ghostwriter out there.

People don't read fiction for entertainment or to escape from reality. People read fiction to see their humanity reflected in another person's character and story.

This is my promise to you. When you read my books, you'll see your own humanity reflected in the characters and stories. I take this commitment to my readers very seriously. My books are an intimate form of communication between us. I would never disrespect my readers by turning that over to a machine or another writer. This is my bond between me and you as my reader.

I write 20,000 words per day as my daily work output. If anyone with a public platform would like to challenge me to prove this in a controlled environment, feel free to contact me on this website's contact page.

I worked as a professional ghostwriter for fifteen years. Now I'm going for the Guinness World Record by writing 700 books over the next ten years and 1400 books over the next twenty years, all originally written by me. See my website for the full book list.

I'm also the author of *Proof for the Existence of God* and the *Crimes Against Fiction* blog. You can find all my nonfiction work at www.crimes-against-fiction.com.

If you have a story idea, or if you would like me to explore a series in more depth, or if you'd like me to explore a character by writing a spinoff series about that character or world, leave me a message on my website's contact page. I answer all reader emails, so ask me anything, tell me what you liked and didn't like, and let me know where you'd like your favorite series to go. I would love to hear your ideas and find out what you'd like to read next.

You can find out more at www.theomann.com or at www.authoraemoran.com.

Also by AE Moran (so far)